HOUR OF NEED

A DCI HARRY MCNEIL NOVEL

JOHN CARSON

DI FRANK MILLER SERIES

Crash Point
Silent Marker
Rain Town
Watch Me Bleed
Broken Wheels
Sudden Death
Under the Knife
Trial and Error
Warning Sign
Cut Throat
Blood from a Stone
Time of Death

Frank Miller Crime Series – Books 1-3 – Box set

MAX DOYLE SERIES

Final Steps
Code Red
The October Project

SCOTT MARSHALL SERIES

Old Habits

HOUR OF NEED

Created with Vellum

For my own younger brother, Derek,
who I never got to meet.
He lived for one month and one day.

ONE

Michelle Naismith put her daughter's book away on the bookshelf and made sure she had her favourite stuffed toy in bed with her, a small rabbit called Jack. She stood looking down at the little form under the covers, feeling like her heart was going to burst with the love she felt. Rachel was only five and Michelle couldn't describe how much love she felt for her daughter.

She stepped over to the window and saw him standing over by the park again.

Him. The man who had been watching the house every night this week.

It was still daylight but she didn't know if the guy had binoculars or a camera with a zoom lens. She closed the curtains.

She'd asked her husband, Clark, to go out and ask him why he was watching the house, but Clark said he didn't want to embarrass himself. Now he was out at the pub and there was a stranger watching the house again.

What if the guy was a pervert? Scoping the house out so he could try and take their daughter? She'd mentioned this to Clark who just brushed her concerns aside. She'd reminded him of sex trafficking and how these deviants would take girls of any age, but it fell on deaf ears as usual.

She went downstairs and saw her son, Dennis, sprawled out on the settee again, his usual place in the evening.

'Rachel's tucked up in bed,' she said.

No answer.

'There's a couple of girls here to see you.'

Her son's head whipped round. Saw only his mother standing there watching him.

'You shouldn't tease a man like that,' he said.

'I just told you Rachel's tucked up in bed. Auntie Linda will be here shortly. We won't be home late. Just a few drinks, that's all.'

'Okay, go then.' He focused on the TV once more.

'No kiss, or anything?'

He blew her a kiss.

'Sixteen and thinks he knows the world,' she said out loud, but Dennis ignored her.

'When will Dad be back?'

'Why? You got a pressing date?'

'Ha ha. No, I just want to Facetime Shona so we can talk about our homework.'

'Make sure your homework gets done. Your dad should be home soon.' She took a light jacket from the back of the chair where she'd left it. Her husband better be home soon. He'd gone straight to the pub and promised he'd be home by seven.

'When will Auntie Linda be here?' Dennis asked.

'Shortly. Why?'

Dennis grinned and looked at her. 'So I can bring Shona in and we can have a drink. Dad will never know. He'll be laid steaming on the couch.'

'I'll know though! Don't be talking like that. Drinking at sixteen indeed.'

Dennis laughed and went back to looking at the TV.

Michelle looked at her watch. She hoped her husband would be here soon. Her sister was due any minute and they wanted to go right out, but she didn't want to leave the kids on their own.

Then they heard shouting coming from outside the front door. Michelle stepped into the hall and saw two figures through the ornate, stained glass window in the front door. The voices were raised and she thought one of them was her husband.

Then she could hear a key turning in the lock. Before the door could be opened, the figures crashed against it and red liquid exploded across the glass on the other side of the door. One of the figures slid down the glass and out of sight below the window.

Michelle was rooted to the spot. The fighting and blood spattering against the glass didn't register for a moment. She stood transfixed, fear coursing through her.

'Mum!' Dennis said, rushing into the hallway. 'What was that?'

Then the mother's instinct kicked in.

'Stay back! Go and call treble nine.'

'And tell them what?'

And tell them what? Michelle didn't have the answer. Two people arguing on her doorstep? A fight going on outside her door? Whatever Dennis told them, the response would be swift. They lived in a decent neighbourhood, so the police would come quickly.

'Let me go and have a look,' he said, meaning to push past his mother, but she put an arm out.

'No. Go upstairs with your sister.' Michelle wondered if the five-year-old girl had heard anything, or whether she was blissfully unaware.

'No! I'm not leaving you down here on your own.'

'Go and call the police!' she screamed, adrenaline coursing through her.

Michelle wasn't looking at him now but focusing on the front door. Maybe she had imagined what had just happened. Her legs felt heavy as she gripped the door handle and turned it. There was something heavy leaning against the door. If it was the pervert from the park, she would show him what it was like to mess with Mama Bear.

She pulled the door open wider and Clark, her husband, fell flat onto the floor, halfway across the threshold.

Michelle screamed then her sister came running up the path.

'Somebody stabbed him!' she shouted at Linda, who saw a figure in dark clothing running away down the street.

Linda knelt down. 'Get towels! Hurry!'

There was a mass of blood running down the front of her husband's shirt.

To Michelle, it looked like Clark's heart had exploded out of his chest.

TWO

DCI Harry McNeil parked his Ford Mondeo in front of the double garage doors and got out, careful not to drop the hot suppers wrapped in newspaper. Inside the large house, his mother was in the living room, the TV on low.

This room was on the second level of the spacious property, with two double windows overlooking the Firth of Forth, affording a view for miles. She turned to face him when he came in.

'Thanks, love,' she said, smiling, the tears dried now but leaving her eyes bright.

'No problem.'

'Alex has been a dear. She's got the kettle on.'

Harry put the suppers down on a small dining table in one corner of the large room. Everything was large about this house, which would have cost probably twice as much in Edinburgh. He walked over to his mother. Only a small lamp illuminated the room so she could see out into the impending dusk as the darkness put an end to the day's show.

'It's beautiful, isn't it?' she said, looking towards the illuminated Forth Rail Bridge in the distance.

'It is. A real testament to engineering. I wonder how long the new Queensferry Crossing will last?'

She turned to face him. 'The old Forth Bridge barely made it fifty years.'

Harry knew his mother was making small talk, skirting the subject. He felt stifled in his suit but at least he'd ditched the black tie when the last of the mourners had gone.

'Here's the tea, Margaret,' Alex said, coming into the room with a tray. She smiled at Harry.

'Thank you, sweetheart. I appreciate your help.'

She set the tray down beside the suppers and they sat down at the table.

'I'm famished,' Harry said, unfolding the newspaper that had been wrapped round the three brown paper packages. 'Two fish suppers and a haggis supper. Magic.'

Margaret tucked into the haggis.

'This fish is terrific,' Alex said.

'It's a great chippy,' Harry agreed, then looked at his mother and saw a tear running down her cheek. He reached out and put a hand on hers.

'I'm not an old hoor, Harry, am I?'

'Jesus, Ma, of course not.'

'I loved Bobby, I really did. And he loved me. Oh, don't get me wrong, I loved your father and when he died, I was devastated, but we were already divorced. It was the drink that got him. I was on my own for a while, but when I met Bobby Dixon, he swept me off my feet. I fell head over heels for him, son.'

'I know. I liked him from the word go.'

Alex was on the other side of Margaret and she put a gentle hand on her arm. 'You've nothing to reproach yourself about, Maggie. You were both widowed, and you both fell in love. And you were with him for two years.'

'I know.' Margaret nodded and sniffed back a tear. 'And Briony's been a comfort, letting me stay here.'

'You both stayed here. Why would she expect you to move out? Your house is still getting work done.'

'I know. There's no rush, she said.'

'Thanks, Harry. You've been a rock for me. Both of you. I don't know what I would have done without you both today. I was dreading the funeral. Knowing you were by my side made all the difference.'

'We're always here for you, Maggie,' Alex said.

'Thank you. I am so glad you two are officially dating. It's not before time. He talked about you all the time.' She smiled at Alex.

'Hello. Still in the room. And I swore you to secrecy, if I remember correctly.'

'I'm your mother. I'm allowed to break promises.'

'Since when?'

'Since you never mind, that's when.'

'Oh, here we go. You'll be showing Alex the photo you have of me getting a bath in the kitchen sink next.'

'I will. And he was sixteen at the time.'

'Months. Sixteen months.'

'I have plenty of photos you can blackmail him with.' Maggie grinned, her eyes still bright but Harry was glad to see the smile on her face.

'I look forward to it,' Alex said.

'Talking of houses, have you finished signing the papers for your flat in Edinburgh?' Margaret looked at each of them in turn.

'Next week, the flat is officially ours,' Harry said.

'And your friend, Frank Miller, was happy to give you a deal?'

'Yes. He made a profit from it, but we still got a bargain.'

'And Vanessa's gone out of your life for good?'

'Yes, Ma, I told you; her house is already sold and she sold her business. She's moved down south.'

'That's good. I liked her but having an ex too close could have led to complications.'

'Well, it's sorted now.' He drank some of the tea that Alex had made. He would have usually preferred to wash the fish down with a beer, but he didn't want a drink. They'd had the wake at a local hotel in Dunfermline, and the bar was free. Enough people had got drunk that day, and he had wanted to stay sober for the sake of his mother.

'You going to be okay staying here, Ma? I mean, in the area.'

'I'm not sure, but I was giving thought to going back up to Inverness. I miss the Highlands.'

Harry ate in silence for a moment, wanting to broach the next subject but hesitant. Then he grabbed the bull by the horns. 'What about Derek?'

Margaret didn't look at her son at first then locked eyes with him. 'He says he's close to finding his own place.'

Harry's face had scepticism written all over it. 'Been looking, has he?'

Margaret looked at the living room door before looking back at her son.

'He can't hear you, Ma, he was too blootered.'

'Oh, Harry, be fair. He helped me with the funeral, something I couldn't have handled myself. He got on well with Bobby.'

'I know that, but he should be standing on his own two feet by now.'

'Why can't you be like your sister? She doesn't judge Derek.'

'Mel's too busy with her own life to know what's going on with Derek.'

'Really?' Margaret wiped her mouth with a napkin. 'Mel might be the manager of a bank department, and mum to two kids, but she always had time to call her brother a couple of times a week. Not like you, Harry.'

Harry could feel his cheeks starting to burn and

wanted to rein his tongue in but his hackles were up. 'If you remember, Derek and I attended the barbeque you had here with Bobby and he took a swing at me. Drunk as usual, and brother or no brother, I would have smacked him if his fist had connected.'

'For God's sake, Harry, you know your wee brother's always had a problem with the drink.'

'And has always had the offer of help, I might add. He enjoys it too much to get help.'

Alex held up a hand. 'Listen, I know that Harry and I are dating and live together, but I feel like I'm a part of your family, Maggie, so please don't take this the wrong way, but I think this has been an emotionally-charged day and everybody is emotionally exhausted, so this might not be the best time to discuss Derek. Just my thoughts.'

'I know, Alex,' Harry said, 'but I'm looking out for my mum. If Derek has his way, he'll bleed her dry.'

'Oh, come on, Harry,' Margaret said, covering up what was left of her supper. 'I know how to look after myself.'

Harry drank some of the coffee. 'And if you do decide to go back to Inverness, will he go with you?'

'I'm not going to see him out on the street. Just like you wouldn't refuse Chance a bed if he came looking for it.'

Harry didn't have an answer but he knew his mother was right. He wouldn't see his own son on the street.

A few minutes of silence ate into their time then Harry's phone rang. 'I have to take this,' he said, getting up from the table and leaving the living room. He stood on the landing outside, looking through a window to the bridge in the distance.

'Okay, what's going on, Karen?'

'Sorry to disturb you this evening, sir, but you said to call if anything big went down,' DI Karen Shiels said.

'It's fine.'

'We got a shout about half an hour ago and when we got to the locus, it was chaos. A man has been stabbed on his doorstep.'

'Christ. Is it fatal?'

'He's clinging to life right now. He's being attended to by a team from Medic One. We have all hands on deck. Armed response is here, just in case.'

'Right. I'm still in Fife but we'll be there as soon as. What's the location?'

'Blackhall.'

'Text Alex the address. We're on our way.'

'Will do.'

He hung up and went back into the room where he could see his mother rubbing at her eyes. Alex had an arm around her shoulders.

'Look, Ma,' he started to say but his mother put up a hand, holding a tissue.

'I don't want to hear any more, Harry. I don't want to fight with you. Not on the day I buried my husband.'

'I don't want a fight. But listen, we have to go.' He looked at Alex. 'We got a shout. There's been a stabbing in Edinburgh. Not fatal but he's fighting for his life.'

Alex gave Margaret a hug before she stood up. 'I can help you clear up.'

'Don't be silly. It's just a few papers. You go. Come back soon.' She gave Alex another hug as they stood. 'Vanessa was never a hugger,' she whispered, then smiled as they parted.

Harry also hugged his mother. 'Whatever goes through your head, Ma, just know that I love you and want what's best for you.'

'I know.'

She saw them downstairs to the front door. 'I'll miss this place, but without Bobby, it's just bricks and mortar. I know this isn't my house but we had some laughs here and Briony is fun.'

'I'll call you over the weekend,' Harry said.

She waved and closed the door as they walked to the front of the garage where he looked out over the dark water of the Forth to the rail bridge in the distance, splendidly lit up.

'A million-dollar view,' he said.

'It is that. But the wind coming from the sea is making me shiver.'

'The wind? Not the prospect of spending the night with me?'

'Alas, that little bit of shock and awe passed a couple of months ago.'

'I'm like a magician; I have plenty of things up my sleeve.'

'Keep that thought, honey. Meantime, get the car running.'

He remotely unlocked the car and they got in.

'I still can't believe you got a Mondeo, and not only that, but an ex-police vehicle.'

'I got them to keep the siren and blues on it. That was an added bonus.' He backed out of the driveway and started driving round to the main road.

'We get to a crime scene and everybody thinks you just arrived in a pool car. Mike the Manky Mondeo we should call it,' Alex said.

'How do you know it's a boy?'

'It's minging, unreliable and makes strange noises from its belly at night.'

'He's not impressed. Mike the *Mad* Mondeo is more like it.' He shook his head. 'Listen to me; naming bloody cars. I used to be normal until I met you.'

'Define *normal*.'

'I used to leave the toilet seat up.'

'That is a normal guy thing right enough.' She turned the heater all the way up although it wasn't warm air coming out of the vents yet. Her phone made a dinging sound as a text arrived.

'I wonder who this is?' she said, fishing in her bag.

'Either Santa Claus letting you know you're now

on the naughty list, or your other boyfriend got his times mixed up.'

'Maybe Santa's my other boyfriend,' she replied, taking her phone out. She read the text. 'Holy cow, that's a nice part of town.'

'I know. Blackhall is very upmarket.'

He floored the car, having activated the blue lights behind the front grill. 'It is. I wonder why somebody was stabbed there.'

Alex said something to him but Harry's mind had slipped to another place. Derek McNeil. He wondered just what his brother's angle was. He had never done anything to help anybody his entire life, and Harry doubted the man would start now.

But then his thoughts turned to a man who had a lot more to worry about. Like trying to make it through the night.

THREE

The street was a scene of chaos when Harry pulled in and found a parking space. An ambulance was still there, beside the other police cars and emergency vehicles. The grey mortuary van was there as well.

'They just pronounced him,' DI Karen Shiels said, approaching them. 'Kate Murphy is here too and the body will be taken to the mortuary. The victim's name is Clark Naismith. Wife is Michelle, son is Dennis. There's also a little five-year-old girl, Rachel. Mrs Naismith's sister was coming to the house too and arrived moments after he was attacked.'

'Were there any witnesses, ma'am?' Alex said.

It was dark and the night had brought with it a lower temperature.

'His wife and kids were in the house. The wife said there was somebody at the door and she was expecting her husband back home. She heard a bang at the door and went to see what was happening and saw two figures fighting. Then blood appeared on the glass in the door window.'

'Did she see anybody?' Harry asked.

'Somebody running away down the street. There's been somebody hanging about, watching the house she says.'

'Right. I'm assuming she's still in the house?'

'Yes, sir. There's a family liaison officer in there with them, keeping them away from the scene. The sister, Linda Hogan was checked out. She had blood on her but it was the victim's.'

There was a crime scene crew standing by, and they all watched as the body was put into a black rubber bag and placed onto a stretcher. Some uniforms helped carry the victim into the mortuary van.

Harry saw the crew from the mobile hospital Medic One, step over to their ambulance, defeat on their faces. He spoke to one of the female nurses, who pointed him to another woman.

'Doctor?'

She turned to him. 'Yes?'

'DCI McNeil. Can I ask you about the victim?'

'Of course. I'm Doctor Kennedy. That was a real bugger.'

'Did he have any chance at all?'

'Slim to none. He had his throat slashed and the weapon entered his chest and I suspect it clipped his heart. The blood loss was too great. We managed to start his heart twice but with less and less to pump, it was struggling to survive.'

'How many stab wounds?'

'Three.'

He looked around at the ambulance. 'What about the female?'

'Nothing. She screamed, apparently, and the attacker ran off.'

'Thanks for trying so hard.'

'We can't win them all, Chief Inspector.' She shrugged and turned back to the ambulance. Harry turned to see some neighbours being nosy on either side of the terraced houses. He waved DC Simon Gregg and DS Eve Bell over.

'Start rounding up the uniforms to canvas the neighbours. I don't care how little they saw, I want them to mention anything. And DI Shiels told me that the wife said she saw somebody hanging about. Ask if anybody else saw him. Sometimes a nosy old bugger walking his dog will have seen something.'

'Yes, sir,' Eve said.

'Simon, get the uniforms to block off the roads leading into here and get uniforms to sweep for a weapon. Get them in the park opposite with dogs. Maybe he disposed of the weapon.'

'I'll get right on it,' Gregg said.

Harry turned to Alex. 'Come on, let's have a word with the widow. I don't suppose anybody's told her about her husband passing?' he said to Karen.

She shook her head, the unspoken inference that he should be the one to do so hung in the air.

'I'll do it then, will I?'

Karen and Alex both agreed that he should.

'Right then, let's go and ruin her day even more.'

They put overshoes on and were guided into the house by a member of the forensics crew, careful not to touch anything around the front door, trying not to step in the blood that had pooled on the concrete step.

Inside, they could hear voices from a back room. A young woman stood pacing, while the FLO was trying her best to calm the woman down. A teenage boy sat in a chair, staring into space. A little girl was asleep on the settee, wrapped in a blanket. Another woman was there, looking dishevelled.

'Mrs Naismith?' Harry asked the pacing woman, thinking it was a better than ninety per cent chance it was her, but he never took it for granted. It might have been a neighbour in giving her moral support.

'Yes. How is he?' She wrung her hands and her eyes silently pleaded with him for good news.

'I'm sorry, but your husband didn't make it. The doctor and her team did everything they could but the wounds were too severe.'

She made a keening noise like an animal and sat down heavily on a chair. The son continued staring into space.

Harry nodded to the young female uniform, silently asking her if she could make some sweet tea.

'I know this is hard,' Alex said, but we have to ask you some questions.'

'Dead? Clark's dead? Oh my God.'

The room was furnished like a living room and Harry wondered if this was the only one. Sometimes a large house had a family room as well, but he didn't know what the difference was. This room had quality furniture as he assumed had the rest of the house.

'Do you know anybody who might want to harm your husband, Mrs Naismith?'

She looked at him, as if she was trying to look right *through* him and then his question registered.

'What? No. Nobody I know of.'

'You told one of my officers that you saw somebody standing outside the house. Can you tell me more about that?'

Michelle looked at him for a moment before something shifted in her brain. 'I saw him standing in the park tonight. Looking right over here, at the house.'

'Could it have been a dog walker, maybe?' Alex said.

Michelle shook her head. 'No. I saw him there before. Every night this week, around the same time. Standing staring at the house.'

'Was it this man you saw stab your husband?' Harry said.

'I didn't see who stabbed him. I'm sorry.'

'Just walk us through what happened.'

She closed her eyes for a moment, raising a paper

20

hanky to her nose. She started to tremble as the sobs came. They waited patiently and then the FLO came in with a tray of steaming mugs.

'What's your name?' Harry asked her.

'Rosie Davis, sir.'

'Sit with Mrs Naismith will you, and I'll do the tea.' Harry stood up and *did the tea* – all he had to do was dish out the mugs. Dennis, the son, didn't want one and just sat staring into space. Rosie took one for Michelle and held it for her, putting an arm around one shoulder, switching attention between the sobbing woman and trying not to spill the tea on the shag pile.

When Michelle was ready, she took the mug in both hands, still clutching the wet hanky.

'Can you tell us what happened, Mrs Naismith?' Alex said, knowing time was of the essence. It was important to get any witness to talk as soon as possible.

Michelle put her mug down on the table at the end of the settee. 'I had put Rachel to bed and had looked out the window to the park across the way, and the man was standing watching the house, so I closed the curtains. I came downstairs and was talking to Dennis when we heard shouting and screaming on the doorstep.'

'And the front door was closed at this point?' Alex said, taking notes.

'Yes. I was expecting Clark to be home any minute, and I thought somebody was shouting at him outside. I saw two figures through the glass then the next thing...

there was a loud bang. They hit the door, hard. Blood spattered up onto the glass.'

'What did you see when you opened the door?' Alex asked.

'My husband was lying there. Gasping.' She nodded to the other woman. 'Linda came running up the path. We were going on a night out. She saw the attacker running away.' She started sobbing quietly again and looked over at the little girl who was still peacefully unaware of what was happening.

'Did you see who stabbed your husband?' Harry asked.

Michelle shook her head. 'No. I only saw his back as he was running away by the time I got the door open.' She locked eyes with him. 'He was dressed in dark clothes like the man in the park, but I know that doesn't mean anything.'

'Maybe if you could sit with one of our profilers who will make a drawing of the man you saw standing in the park.'

She nodded. Then they watched as the teenage boy got up and left the room.

'I'll go and see to him,' Rosie said. She got up and went after him.

Harry nodded and looked at Michelle again. 'I will need you to come to the station tomorrow and give us a formal statement, Mrs Naismith. Just a formality. Officer Davis will pick you up and bring you in.'

'Okay, I'll be there.'

Harry told her they were based in the old HQ building at Fettes and they agreed on a time.

'How about you, Mrs Logan? Can you tell us what happened?'

'It's Miss Logan.' She gathered her thoughts for a moment. 'Michelle and I were going out for a few drinks tonight. I got out of the Uber but he had stopped a few houses up. I walked towards the house and saw a man run off. Then Michelle screamed. When I got there, Clark was lying on the floor, bleeding heavily.'

'Was he coming home from work?' Harry asked Michelle.

'No, he was coming home from the pub. He went for a couple after work with some friends.'

'What pub?'

'Sometimes they go to the Oak Inn, on St John's Road.'

'Would he have got a bus or a taxi home?'

'If they were just having a couple, then he would probably have got dropped off by one of his co-workers. They didn't all drink a lot.'

'We'll have to find whoever dropped him off,' he said, then he stood up and left the house with Alex.

It was chilly outside as they made their way carefully past the spot where Clark Naismith had just died. The mortuary van was gone.

'What's your gut saying, Alex?' Harry asked, realising that they were both still dressed for a funeral.

'It wasn't random, that much is obvious. The man

in the park? There has to be a link, unless it was a man with a dog and she couldn't see the dog and just has an overactive imagination. Maybe Clark got himself into some shady deal or something. We need a complete rundown on his background.'

'Which we will get tomorrow morning. I'll get Eve Bell onto it first thing.'

DC Simon Gregg approached them; a young man who towered over Harry. 'We have a witness who saw a man running down the street, sir,' he said. 'He didn't get a look at his face but he was slim and could run fast. Then he heard a car's tyres screeching, which means he either had help or he parked around the corner. DI Shiels has uniforms knocking on doors to see if anybody saw or heard a car around the corner.'

'Good work. Tomorrow we can see if any businesses have CCTV out on the main road.'

They made their way through the uniforms. 'I want a full background check on them both. Find out if she works and if so, where.'

'Will do.'

They were at the scene for another couple of hours before they left. Harry was silent as he got behind the wheel of the Mondeo.

'You okay?' Alex asked.

'What? Oh, yes. I was just thinking about my brother. Christ, I almost forgot I had a brother until my mum brought his name up again. Typical he wants to stay with her again.'

'You've never mentioned him before the funeral.'

'There was nothing to talk about; he was out of my life.'

'I'd like to see your sister again. She seems like she would be great fun, in the right circumstances.'

'Mel's fine. I haven't seen her in ages because she works and has the kids. The timing's never right.' He started up the car and drove slowly away from the scene, heading towards Queensferry Road and home to Comely Bank.

'You forget I'm a detective too.'

'What's that supposed to mean?'

'That I can see right through your drivel, Harry McNeil.'

'Oh, I see how it goes; we've been dating for a couple of months and now all of a sudden, you can see right through me?'

'No,' she said smiling, 'I've always been able to see right through you.'

He laughed. 'So you think, lady.'

'Anyway, I think there's more to it than meets the eye. Why you don't see more of your sister.'

He drove down the road in silence for a moment. 'We had words, a long time ago. Many years ago, about my dad's drinking. My dad was a police officer as you know, and like a lot of coppers before him, he drank a lot. I used to go drinking with him when I first started on the force. And when I say drinking, I mean we got blootered. And all of a sudden, I was the bad guy, the enabler. My mum divorced him before my probation was up.'

'How did your dad feel about that?'

'He was upset. He begged my mum not to go through with the divorce, and she said she wouldn't if he would stop drinking. He did try. I thought my mum was going to give him a second chance but then he started drinking again. But by God, he was a happy drunk my old man. We had such a good laugh. My mum said he couldn't be trusted, and she was also pissed off at me for drinking with him.'

'Plenty of couples get divorced.'

'True, but my mum and my sister ganged up on me. I'm the oldest, I should have known better. Derek was too young to drink, so it all fell on me. It wouldn't have been so bad, but my dad moved into a little council flat, and he was having a good time, until one night he went out drinking and came home and had a heart attack. They didn't find his body for three days.'

'Oh God, Harry, I'm sorry.'

'Oh, don't be,' he said, turning into their street. He found a parking spot and turned the engine off. 'My father was a grown man who made his own decisions. He decided drink was better for him than being married to my mum. If he had chosen her, he might have still been alive.'

'Still. He was your dad.'

'Yep. And I miss him every day.'

'Where do you think your mum will go?' Alex asked when they were up in their flat.

'I honestly have no idea. More to the point, where will my brother go?'

'He can always stay here. Until he gets on his feet.'

Harry walked over to her and put a finger over her lips. 'Your heart is in the right place, but promise me you'll never utter those words again. That and *Do you like your bacon crispy?*'

He took his finger away and kissed her.

'I only asked about the bacon one time.'

'Some things are only meant to be said once. Like the offer to have my brother come stay here.'

'I was only saying.'

'I know. That's why I'll let you off the hook this time.'

'Or else what, Mister Bigshot?'

'Or else you might not get any of this tonight.' He ran his hands up and down in front of himself.'

'Oh please. I can have that any time I want.'

'Okay. Go ahead and test me.'

Alex rolled her eyes. 'Please can you make wild, passionate love to me tonight, Harry?'

'Well, seeing how you put it like that...'

'You lasted what, five seconds?'

'Don't be saying that around the office.'

He took his black tie off and undid the button on his shirt. 'What do you reckon to this attacker?' he said, putting the kettle on.

'Professional job,' Alex replied.

'Agreed. Nice neighbourhood like that, it's not likely somebody would just walk up to a stranger on their doorstep and knife him. No signs of robbery. No getting into the house. Just a few quick jabs and it's all over.' He made two mugs of green tea.

'Let's drink that in bed. Maybe watch some TV.'

They took it through to the room and got changed for bed.

'What did your mum's husband do for a living?' Alex asked as they were settled.

'He owned several businesses.'

'And now your mum owns them, I assume?'

'What are you getting at?' Harry said, flipping through channels and settling on an animal documentary.

'I'm not getting at anything. I was just curious. I feel sorry for Margaret though; she lost both her husbands, albeit under different circumstances. Your dad died of a heart attack and Bobby drowned in the Forth, his features eaten away.'

'He would have liked you,' Harry said.

'Really?'

'Yes. He couldn't stop talking when the TV was on either, apparently.'

She whacked him with a pillow.

FOUR

Harry came back into the flat with a carrier bag, the smell of coffee hitting his nostrils.

'You're up early,' he said, seeing Alex sitting on the settee with her laptop on her knees.

'I couldn't sleep. I was too wired after yesterday.'

'Why? Were you binge watching *Hey Arnold* on Netflix again? I told you to put the light out last night, otherwise you'd be knackered this morning, but what do I know?'

'Like I could watch cartoons with your snoring.'

'You told me that was an endearing feature.'

'I lied. Just go and get your coffee. We'll discuss the finer things about snoring later.'

He put the bag in the kitchen and took his jacket off. It was getting warm outside, but there was still a chilly wind. He added some milk to the coffee.

'I saw our next-door neighbour in Waitrose,' he shouted through.

'Should I be worried?'

'Not unless you're allergic to cats,' Harry said, coming into the living room with a mug of coffee and a bowl of cereal.

'Cats? Is this your subtle way of telling me you want a cat?'

'Nothing wrong with cats. We had cats when I was growing up.'

'No, don't get me wrong, I love cats too. We had them when I was growing up, but when you said you wanted to hear the pitter patter of tiny feet one day, I sort of assumed you meant a baby.'

'Cats have babies.' He sat down at the small dining table by the window.

'You're skating on thin ice here, Harry McNeil. Toying with a woman like that.'

He laughed. 'I'm kidding, beautiful lady. Mia asked if we could look after her cat while she's away.'

'How long for?'

'A week. He's a great wee guy. Every time she's opened her door and I've been coming or going, he runs out and wraps himself around my legs. A bit like how you wrap me round your little finger.'

'I wish. This is the same *Me Harry, You Jane* we're talking about?'

'I don't treat you like that.' He drank some coffee and got tucked into his cereal.

'In front of her, you do. Mia.'

'Rubbish.'

She looked over the top of her laptop at him. 'If we had a spider plant, you'd be ripping a leaf off and covering yourself with it as you stand bare-chested on the landing.'

He started to grin then the smile dropped. 'Hey, wait a minute; don't spider plants have narrow leaves?'

'Yes. Just think yourself lucky I didn't say jaggie nettles. Small and painful. Like me.'

'I can see this conversation went down a road I didn't expect it to. But how about it? Looking after Sylvester?'

'Sure. Why not? You can tell her that would be fine. When do we have to start going over to see him?'

'Actually, she asked if he could stay here. Would that be okay?'

'What if he thinks the settee is his big scratching post?'

'Mia said he doesn't do that sort of thing.'

'Well, she would, wouldn't she? That would hardly be a selling point. But of course he can. As long as she doesn't have a Tweetie Pie as well.'

'Just the cat. I'll let you tell her later that it's okay.'

'Right. I'd better get ready,' she said, closing the laptop. 'I'll shower first then we can get over to the office. I hope Michelle Naismith remembers to bring her son.'

'I already called Rosie, the FLO. She's back on duty again today. She said she's bringing them down.'

'Good.' She walked out of the room with her laptop and Harry finished his coffee and cereal. He was about to sit down to watch some morning news when his mobile phone rang. He didn't recognise the number, but answered it anyway.

'McNeil.'

'Harry, good morning!' the voice on the other end said.

Harry recognised his brother. 'Derek.'

'Don't sound so cheery,' Derek said, laughing.

'I'm getting ready for work. You know, the thing that brings in a little pay packet every month. You should try it.'

'Aw, come on now.' There was still a hint of bonhomie in his voice, but it was hanging by a thread. 'Mum told me you got called away last night. Sorry I wasn't there to say goodbye.'

'You were in your room, blootered, in no state to say goodbye. I looked in but not even a pipe band could have woken you.'

'Aye, I know that. But considering we had to bury one of our own, it's reasonable to expect a man to have a drink or three.'

'Just remember that *Drink Canada Dry* is an advertising slogan, not a challenge.'

'Listen, Harry, I know you and I have been through the mill the last few years...'

'Is that what you call it? *Through the mill?* I would call it you being a sponger.'

'That's a bit strong.'

'Is it now? A hard day's work would kill you.'

'I know you're angry, but Mel was pleased to see me.'

'Our sister sometimes sees the world through rose-coloured glasses. I, however, see you for what you are.'

'Aw, Jesus, Harry, get off your high horse.'

Harry could feel his temper rising but he wasn't going to let his brother get the better of him. 'Look, Derek, I wish you all the best, but maybe you shouldn't call anymore.'

'Fine. I won't call you again. Not even to discuss my thoughts on why I think Bobby was murdered.'

'Murdered?' Harry replied, but he was talking to dead air.

FIVE

'Murdered,' Harry said as he stepped out of Alex's Audi.

'Harry, stop. Derek was probably playing with your head.'

'Why would he say that though?'

'Because he's a moron.' They walked through the car park of the old Lothian and Borders HQ where their office was located.

'Luckily it doesn't run in the family.' He looked at her for a moment. 'Feel free to jump in anytime to agree with me.'

'I'm staying neutral.'

'I think I just got insulted by my girlfriend.'

She grinned at him. 'I hope Simon's got the kettle on.'

'I hope he's out of his bloody pit.'

Upstairs, the coffee thing hadn't materialised.

Harry ended up putting on the kettle when he saw what state Gregg was in.

'Late night?' he said.

'I had a date, but with working late, I thought it wouldn't happen. But she still wanted to meet and I went to her place. I wasn't drunk but we sat and talked until the wee hours.'

'Okay. Good. I'm glad I have your full attention.'

DI Karen Shiels had put things on the whiteboard while DS Eve Bell was sitting in front of a computer.

Harry made the coffees. 'Right, let's get this ball rolling,' he said. 'Eve? Tell me what background you have on the Naismith family.'

'Yes, sir,' Eve replied, clacking the keyboard. 'Michelle and Clark Naismith were married six years ago.'

Harry held up a hand. 'The son's sixteen. Did they have him before they got married?'

'That's not an unusual situation, sir, he's her son from her first marriage,' Alex said.

'I'm not saying it is, but it took me by surprise. Carry on.'

'No. Second marriage for both of them,' Eve said, reading off the screen.

'Jealous ex-spouse?' Karen said.

'Could be. Are they both on the scene?'

'Clark's ex-wife lives in Fife. Dunfermline. Michelle's former husband is an ex-soldier. He lives in Glasgow, which doesn't preclude him.'

'Okay. But we need somebody to talk to them. Find out where they were last night. You got addresses for them?'

'Yes, sir,' Eve said. 'I already printed them out.'

'We can talk to them later. I'll give DCI Jimmy Dunbar a call, see if he can locate the ex-husband for us and have a word. Alex and I are going through to Glasgow tonight and staying overnight. We can arrange for the ex-husband to get interviewed if he's around.'

'Not like the old days, eh, sir?' Karen said.

'What do you mean?'

'Now we're one big police force, we can ask another division to find somebody and we can go interview them. Not like before, when we had to do it ourselves and ask for their cooperation.'

'You make me feel like I should be blowing out candles on a cake and walking out with my token pocket watch. I might have one or two grey hairs creeping in but retirement is far from round the corner.'

'No, I didn't mean anything,' Karen replied, feeling her face go red.

'He's winding you up, hen,' a voice said from the doorway. They all turned around to see who was there.

'He's right, I was,' Harry said, grinning at Karen. 'You remember DI Ronnie Vallance?'

'Yes, I do,' she said, a slight smile on her face.

The detective was older than Harry, bigger both in

height and weight. He had a neatly-trimmed beard and his smile was wide. He walked into the room and let the door close behind him.

'Welcome, Ronnie. These are the other members of my team. Ronnie will be on our team from now on.' He made the introductions.

'You didn't tell us we were getting a new member, sir,' Alex said.

'I only heard about it yesterday. I wasn't expecting our intrepid DI to appear until Monday.'

'I was expecting a lie-in, a good breakfast and then a few pints this afternoon until I got the call from Jeni Bridge last night to get my arse down here this morning. The first Saturday I've worked in a long time.'

Commander Jeni Bridge was in charge of Police Scotland, Edinburgh Division.

'I assume she gave you a rundown of the case?' Harry said.

'She did indeed.' He was holding a cup of coffee and put it down so he could take his jacket off.

'Tell us all where you came from,' Harry said. 'For the benefit of those who don't know you.'

'Gayfield Square. CID. I was approached by the head of CID himself, Super Percy Purcell. He said they wanted more hands in this MIT and would I be interested? I jumped at the chance. Specially to work with this man again.' He grinned at Harry.

'One of the few coppers who doesn't hate me for being in Professional Standards,' Harry said.

'That's because I kept my nose clean and I always had respect for DCI McNeil, especially since we worked together before.'

'I have a tight wee team here, Ronnie. I'm sure you'll fit right in.'

'I have to admit, I feel like a wee laddie going to school for the first time. I've heard good things about you lot, and I thought I had big boots to fill.'

'Nobody's boots to fill. We needed another body on the team and I had a talk with Superintendent Purcell. He fast-tracked the request.'

'I appreciate that.'

'Right, let's get back to work. Where were we?' Harry said.

'The ex-partners of the Naismiths,' Eve said.

'Yes.' Harry filled him in. 'Glasgow may be tomorrow, depending on whether we can nail this ex down to interview him. We're expecting the victim's wife to come in for an interview shortly. With her son, Dennis.'

'Is he going to be interviewed separately?' Vallance asked.

'Yes. I want her permission to do that,' Harry said. 'I want to hear what he has to say without his mother being there.'

'Good idea. Meantime, do we have anything from witnesses?'

'Nothing so far, but uniforms are going around again this morning. Sometimes they won't remember seeing something in all the excitement but will remember something later. Plus, they didn't get an answer at every door last night.'

Eve was tapping away at the computer then she turned to Harry. 'We do have another witness who saw somebody running down the street and getting into a car before it roared away. He got in the passenger side.'

'An accomplice,' Karen said.

'We know which way he left, so we can get local CCTV,' Alex said.

'Can you get onto that?' Harry said, then one of the phones rang. He answered it and spoke to the caller before hanging up. 'That was the front desk. Mrs Naismith and her son are here and they're being shown up to the interview rooms. I'll take Karen and we'll do the interviews. Simon, you can join DI Shiels. Eve, you're with me. Alex, can you carry on doing the background research with DI Vallance? Bring him up to speed.'

'Will do.'

Outside in the corridor, Harry stood and talked to his team members. 'Go over what happened last night. That laddie was quiet, and we all know what shock can do to somebody but I want to hear it from the horse's mouth, as it were.'

Inside interview room 1, Michelle Naismith sat on the chair, a uniform standing just inside the door. Her perfume was wafting around the windowless room and Harry decided it was expensive. Nothing like the stuff he used to buy his wife from Pound-stretcher.

'Mrs Naismith, thank you for coming along this morning. Did the family liaison officer drive you here?'

Michelle nodded. 'She did, thank you.' There was a hanky in her right hand that she used to dab at her bloodshot eyes.

'Would you like a tea or anything to drink?'

'No, I'm fine thanks.'

Harry nodded to the uniform who left the room and he sat down opposite Michelle, with Eve Bell at his side. The cameras above them were recording.

He did the formal introductions for the cameras.

'Since we talked last night, have you recalled anything else that can be of assistance to us?' Harry spoke in a gentle voice.

'Nothing. I've been running it through my mind, over and over.'

'You said you saw the man running away,' Eve said. 'Can you remember anything else about him?'

Michelle shook her head. 'Just what I told the officer last night. Dark clothes, dark hair, average build. Young. He ran like a young man.'

'I'd like to ask you about your husband now, Mrs Naismith,' Harry said. 'Now you've had time to think, do you know why anybody would want to harm him?'

'No. We lived a simple life. He worked in the bank as a loans officer. Hardly a reason for somebody to want him dead.'

'Which bank?'

'The Scottish National out at Gogar.'

'Did he work with the public?'

'No. Loans were applied for and he would give them approval or not. But he didn't work with people who walked in off the street. He dealt with corporate clients.'

'Did he say if anybody was upset with him recently?'

'He didn't discuss his work with me, and I liked it that way. But even if I wanted him to, he couldn't. He signed confidentiality papers so he couldn't discuss cases out of the bank. It was all boring stuff anyway, I imagine.'

'What about his personal life?' Eve asked.

'What do you mean?'

'You said he was at the pub last night. Did he ever mention getting into an argument with somebody outside of work?'

'No. Clark didn't go fighting. He was such a gentle man. He was a happy drunk, but he didn't get drunk very often.'

'He was coming in around seven last night, after being at the pub. We checked; there wasn't any trouble last night. Is that a usual thing for him, to go to the pub on a Friday evening?'

'Yes. He went drinking with some friends from work.'

'Do you know any of their names?' Eve asked.

'It was just some colleagues. One of them was his best friend, Tommy Gallagher. They worked in the same department.'

'Would you have any contact details for him?'

'His number might be in Clark's phone.'

'Right,' Harry said. 'We have that. I'll get one of our people to check on that. Meantime, can I ask if you have any financial problems?'

'No. We were doing fine. The mortgage was going to be paid off early. We have savings.'

'What do you do for a living?' Harry said. He already knew the answer but wanted to hear it from her.

'I'm a home help. I work for a company that sends us to help out elderly clients. With shopping, picking up medicine. Stuff like that. I only work a couple of days a week, just to get out of the house. Now that Rachel is in primary school.'

'Where is she now?' Eve asked.

'One of your other officers is looking after her.'

'We'll need details of your job,' Harry said.

'I can write that down.'

Eve handed her a pen and pad and she wrote her employer's details down.

'Where's my son?' Michelle asked.

'He's with one of my senior officers now. Don't worry, he's being taken care of,' Harry said.

'You'll see him after he's spoken to our team.'

Harry finished the interview and Eve took

Michelle to wait in another room.

'What do you think?' Alex asked him as he went into the incident room.

'I think she's hiding something. I can't wait to hear what the laddie had to say for himself.' He had just poured himself a coffee when Ronnie Vallance and Simon Gregg came in, followed by Eve.

'Well?' Harry said.

'Ignorant wee bastard. No' you, boss, that laddie,' Vallance said.

'I didn't think you were talking about me. What happened?'

'Why don't we sit down and watch the show?'

Harry turned to Karen Shiels. 'Can you bring up the recorded interview?'

'I can do that.'

Harry joined Vallance over by the kettle as he made coffee for everybody. 'He was giving you attitude, I take it?'

'Christ, Harry, if the little sod didn't have his mother as an alibi, I would be wanting to put the cuffs on him right now. Bloody cheeky wee sod. He doesn't even seem to care that his old man's gone.'

'Shock affects everybody in different ways, Ronnie, you know that.'

'Aye, I do that, but this laddie takes things to a whole new level. Cold, that's how I would describe him. But you'll see for yourself.'

As the others grabbed their coffee, Karen Shiels got

the interview up on a monitor. They sat round the screen on chairs, waiting for the show to start.

'What do you call it when a big family just bought a TV?' Vallance said.

They all looked at him.

'Contraception.'

They all groaned in unison.

'Roll the tape.'

SIX

'Can you state your name for the record?' Ronnie Vallance asked the teenager.

'Dennis Naismith.'

'Thanks, Dennis. My name's DI Ronnie Vallance and this is DC Simon Gregg.'

'When can I go home?' Dennis said.

'Well, we've only just got in here, son, so it's going to be a little while.'

'I'm not your son.'

'Figure of speech,' Gregg said.

Dennis looked at him. 'It speaks.'

'I'm going to ask you to keep this civil,' Vallance said. 'I know you're upset about your dad dying, but we're trying to find out who killed him.'

'Stepdad.' Dennis sat back in the chair with his arms folded, as if he was challenging the two detectives to play head games with him.

'I want you to tell me in your own words what happened last night,' Vallance said.

'I already told that daft bint who's at our house. The one who drove us here this morning. God, she's an awful driver.'

Vallance clenched his jaw before speaking. 'Listen, son, I don't want to hear you talking like that about one of my officers.'

'Well. God's sake, she almost hit a bus.'

'Even if that's true, you're here in one piece.'

'Are you calling me a liar?' Dennis said and shot forward in the chair, slapping his hands down on the table.

'Nobody's calling you anything,' Gregg said. 'Just answer the inspector's questions.'

'Got you talking for him now, has he?'

Vallance took a deep breath and let it out slowly. 'This is going to take a lot longer if you just sit there and give us backchat.'

Dennis locked eyes with Vallance before sitting back in the chair. 'Get on with it then.'

'I asked you to tell us what happened last night.'

'I was in the living room watching TV. My mum was upstairs putting Rachel to bed and when she came down, we heard a commotion at the door.'

'What sort of commotion?' Gregg asked.

Dennis turned his head slowly towards him. 'A fight. Is *commotion* too big a word for you?'

Gregg stared back. 'Just carry on.' The words *you little bastard* weren't added but were clearly inferred.

Dennis looked back at Vallance as if he'd expected the older man to have fallen asleep while he took the eye off the ball for a moment.

'There was banging against the front door. Then nothing. I wanted to go out there but my mum wouldn't let me. She went and opened the door and my dad was leaning against the doorway and he fell in. My auntie Linda came up and tried to help him. I was looking from the living room door.'

'Then what?' Vallance asked.

'She started screaming and called the police.'

'Did you see your dad's attacker?' Gregg asked.

'Nope.'

'How did your mum and dad get along?'

'What do you mean?'

'Did they argue?' Gregg asked.

'Sometimes.'

'What did they fight about?' Vallance asked.

Dennis shrugged. 'Money. Sometimes when my dad came in late from the pub.'

'Did your dad ever hit your mum?'

'No. Not in front of me.'

'Did your mum ever hit your dad?'

'No, of course not.'

'Did your dad ever hit you?' Vallance asked. 'Like, if you were being cheeky to him or giving him attitude or anything?'

'No.'

'How long was he your stepdad for?' Vallance asked.

'About ten years. Something like that.'

'Did you ever hear your dad talking on the phone to somebody? Maybe talking sternly?'

'No. What do you think I do? Eavesdrop on my parents?' He sneered at him.

'I'm not saying that. I'm trying to establish if anybody would want to hurt your father or whether it was somebody just walking along the street who decided to stab him.'

'No, I didn't listen in on any phone calls, alright?'

'You mother said she saw somebody watching the house the past few nights. Did you see that man?'

'The perv watching us? Yeah, I saw him. I took a photo of him.'

'Why didn't you tell us?' Gregg said.

'You never asked.'

'Now listen here, sonny. As I just said, we're trying to catch your father's killer so a wee bit of co-operation wouldn't go amiss.'

'I don't know anything, I didn't see anything. Okay? I want to see my mum now.'

Vallance got the boy to send him a copy of the photo he'd taken then ended the interview and they all left the room.

SEVEN

'It could be shock,' Eve Bell said, turning away from the monitor.

Harry and Vallance looked at each other. 'We'll give him the benefit of the doubt, will we?'

'I've got twin laddies about his age, and I know they haven't experienced their dad being murdered, but any other kid I've met who lost a parent didn't act like that,' Vallance said. 'Thank God I've got an older daughter as well.'

'As Eve said, it could be shock. But bear in mind that this wasn't his father, but his stepfather, and sometimes, that makes a difference. Where is he now, Ronnie?'

'His mother has him. The FLO is taking them home and she'll be staying with them, and I've ordered an armed patrol to be outside for the rest of the day, unless they get a shout.'

'Good,' Karen Shiels said. 'We're working on the assumption that this was a hit but we can't be sure.'

'I want everything that forensics has so far. Prints from the car. Alex? You come up with anything from the CCTV hunt yet?'

'We did. A witness saw a red Astra go along Gardiner Road at high speed, then turn right onto Seaforth Terrace, which is the main road. Another part of the main road is called Marischal Place, and there's a little independent store there with a camera outside. It caught the Astra and when it goes past, there are clearly two men inside. We could make out two figures.'

'Number plate?'

'The lab is analysing it now to see if they can blow the picture up but they haven't got back to us.'

'Probably get a better picture using a toaster,' Vallance said. 'They can send sharper pictures from Mars than you get from some of those CCTV cameras.'

'Isn't that the truth. But Naismith worked office hours, so we'll get to the bank first thing Monday morning to talk to his colleagues. The post-mortem is scheduled for Monday too. We'll collate any info from the forensics lab. We'll regroup first thing Monday morning after we get the interviews done with the exes tomorrow. Thanks for coming in, team.'

Outside in the corridor, Ronnie Vallance was standing. 'The team are a nice bunch, Harry. I appreciate you putting my name forward.'

'No problem, mate. We worked well together a few years back, and Jeni Bridge said she wanted more bodies on the team. Sometimes, we'll be called to support a smaller MIT somewhere else in Scotland, so she wants a strong team here when the other members are away. You and Karen have good experience and the rest of the team will have your back.'

Vallance smiled. 'Aye, well, Angie and the boys are fair chuffed about my move. Angie might think I'm a real detective for once.'

'I'm sure you're selling yourself short there.'

'Maybe. But we're going on a date night for the first time in ages. Which is great since the boys are at an age where they can look after themselves.'

'I'm looking forward to spending the night in a nice hotel, too.'

'Oh aye, somebody mentioned you were seeing Alex now.'

'Long story short, she was using my spare room, and we got together.'

'Good for you, Harry. You deserve some fun after what Morag put you through.'

'Water under the bridge now, pal. I'm happy. We both are.' He looked round as Alex came out of the room. 'Talk of the devil.'

'I thought my ears were burning.'

'Harry was just telling me how happy you're making him,' Vallance said.

'Don't tell her that. Her head will never fit through the door.'

Alex nudged him. 'And we bought a flat together. Maybe one day I can get him to make an honest woman of me.'

'Arrest you, you mean?' Harry said.

'Indeed, I do not.'

'And when you're a DCI one day, there will be two DCI McNeils,' Vallance said. 'The Edinburgh underworld won't know what's hit them.'

'You tell him, sir.'

'Oh, jeez, no *sir* allowed unless it's in front of the team. Harry and I go way back.'

Alex looked at Harry and he smiled.

'Don't worry, Ronnie is one of the good guys.'

Vallance looked puzzled.

'Never mind, I'll explain one day,' he said. 'Come on, Alex, we have to get going. The party's at seven and I don't want to be late.'

'I'll see you first thing Monday morning,' Vallance said. 'Enjoy the rest of your weekend.'

They went down to Harry's Mondeo and his phone rang. He tossed her the keys and jumped into the passenger seat. He stared at the screen for a few seconds, the name on the display conjuring up images he didn't want to let loose. All of them involved his brother in various stages of pain.

'If this is to tell me about one of your wild conspiracy theories, I'm not interested,' he said after answering. Alex started the car and drove out of the station car park.

'Harry, just hear me out, okay? Please.'

His brother wasn't exactly begging but Harry felt that this was already lined up in the queue.

'You want me to listen to you? That would be a first, Derek.'

'Aw come on. You know I didn't know those guys were dodgy.'

'Dodgy? One of them had the nickname *Axeman*.'

Derek laughed. 'Oh aye. Like *the Axeman Cometh*.'

'Now look, whatever it is you want to say, say it, and then get out of my life.' Harry could feel his face going red.

'Easy there, brother. I just wanted to reiterate that I think Bobby Mitchell was murdered.'

'What proof do you have?'

'Ah, there's the rub; I don't exactly have proof. Just a theory. But a good one, mind.'

'Is it the same people who murdered JFK?'

'Harry, I want to meet up with you to discuss this.'

'Don't hold your breath,' Harry said and hung up.

'Do you think you'll ever reconcile with Derek?' Alex asked.

'Too much water has passed under the bridge for that. I gave him many chances, but enough was enough.'

'And this thing with him claiming Bobby was murdered?'

'He's just working an angle. My brother could persuade the birds out of the trees.'

'Try not to let it ruin our night though.'

'I won't. I'm looking forward to seeing Jimmy Dunbar and young Robbie Evans again.' But there was one niggling little thought that wouldn't go away; what if Derek wasn't making it up?

EIGHT

'I feel bushed,' Alex said as they got in. She took her shoes off and plonked herself down onto the settee.

'Don't get too comfortable there. I want to get through sharp and get settled into the hotel room before tonight.'

'I suppose. I just feel like a nap.' She held out a hand for him to pull her up.

'You're getting old. And please don't say you need a nap when we're booting it along the M8.'

'I'll be fine. I'll have a coffee before we go. It was just a drain yesterday, being at the funeral.'

'I know,' he said, pulling her close. 'I hate to see my mother so upset again. She was gutted when my dad died, and to see her bury another husband wasn't easy.'

'Poor thing. You should give her a call, just to make sure she's alright.'

'I will.'

'I'm going to finish packing my suitcase.'

'If you give me five minutes, I'll get my spanner out so I can disconnect the kitchen sink.'

'You're so funny, McNeil. But it's easy for you; all you have to do is throw a clean pair of underpants and a toothbrush into a carrier bag and you're off.'

'There's a lot to be said about travelling light.'

She laughed and left the living room. Harry sat at the small dining table that overlooked the bowling club down below and dialled his mother's number.

'Hi, Ma,' he said after she answered.

'Hello, Harry,' she replied and he could detect an icy tinge in her voice. Not quite frosty, but like a coldness in a winter sky. He waited for the lashing he felt was coming.

'How you doing today?'

'Oh, I've not only had my heart broken by my husband dying, but by my own flesh and blood.'

'Derek not done hoovering today?' He immediately regretted the words as soon as he'd said them, but he'd known his brother's name would be popping up any second.

His remark was followed by an intake of breath, like somebody might do when they were about to let out a scream, getting their lungs filled before letting go.

'I'm glad you can mock your brother like this, Harry. I never thought I'd live to see this day, but there you have it. You never know what's around the corner.'

And there we have it, he thought, the psychology.

Derek had obviously gone running to Mummy to get her on his side, and it had worked.

'What's he been spouting now?' *Did he tell you he thinks your husband was murdered?*

'He just wants to reconnect with you, that's all. Is that so bad for a brother to want to be friends with his own flesh and blood?'

'It depends on what he wants.'

'Oh, Harry, can you just stop being pig-headed for a moment?' The volume control had been given a tweak, just in case he hadn't heard her the first time.

'I really don't know what you want me to say. I tried with Derek a long time ago. He blew it.'

'Everybody deserves a second chance, son. I gave him a second chance.'

'How many second chances do you give somebody though, Ma? Where do you draw the line?'

'You do whatever it takes. He's your brother. Why can't you just meet him for a pint one night? He just told me that's what he wants more than anything.'

'And talk about what? We have nothing in common.'

'Do you want to see me in an early grave? Is that what you want? I'm going to pick up Bobby's ashes next week. There are things I wished I'd said to him before he died. Like, how much I loved him. He knew, and we always told each other, but I wish I had told him on the day he left the house and never came home. Don't live with regrets, son.'

Replies came at him like stars came at the bridge window on the *Enterprise* but he kept his mouth shut. He looked down at the bowling club, where he and Alex might have stepped in for a few drinks that night if they weren't going to the party. 'Fine,' he heard himself say, not quite believing the words were coming out.

'Fine what?'

'Fine, *Mother*.'

'Don't be a smartarse, Harry.'

'Fine, I'll take the whining wee brat out for a pint. But he can come over here.'

'He doesn't have a car.'

'You do. Bobby did. Let him drive Bobby's Jag.'

'Bobby would roll over in his urn if he knew Derek was behind the wheel of his beloved car.'

'Maybe Bobby will see his way to sitting in the passenger seat with him then.' *Christ, Harry, what are you trying to do?* 'Sorry, that came out wrong.'

'There was a right way to say that, was there?'

'Sorry. But my offer stands; he can come through here if he wants a beer.'

'He can hardly have a few beers if he's driving now, can he?'

'He'll be fine if he has one, two tops.' The last thing Harry wanted was his brother coming through for a sesh. One of them would be getting battered, and it wasn't Harry.

'I'll drive him to the train station. It's only a five-minute drive from here,' Margaret said.

'I'll tell you when I'm available.'

There was silence for a moment, each of the fighters retreating to their corner where they could still size each other up, but Harry knew he would never win this fight. Better to go out with some dignity than go down like a burning Spitfire.

'I'll let you know next week.'

'Thank you, son. I'll give him some cash so he can buy you a pint.'

'You don't have to. I can stretch myself to buying him a pint.' He deliberately used the singular.

'He'll be so pleased.'

'I've got to go, Ma. I'll speak to you soon.'

He disconnected the call and felt anger at himself for being so weak.

Then he went through to the bedroom to finish packing his carrier bag.

NINE

'There they are!' DCI Jimmy Dunbar said, smiling and walking across the dance floor to where Harry and Alex were standing. Alex was holding a box wrapped in shiny paper with a card taped to the top.

'Good to see you again, Jimmy,' Harry said as they shook hands.

'Likewise, my friend.' He turned to Alex. 'I'm so glad you could make it. It means a lot.'

'We wouldn't miss it for the world, Jimmy.' She gave him a peck on the cheek.

'Let me introduce you to the missus. She's around here somewhere.' He looked around the function room. A band was on the stage at the far end and the room was filled with people talking and laughing, sitting at round tables like they were at a wedding reception. Decorations hung on the walls, with banners congratulating the happy couple on their twenty-fifth wedding anniversary.

'There she is. Dancing with our best man. He maybe thinks he's in with a chance but he's twenty-five years too late.' He grinned at them both.

'Is Robbie here?' Alex asked.

'Aye. We invited the wee reprobate. He came along on his own. I think his plus one was his mother but she took ill or something.'

'He's a good catch for somebody,' Alex said, laughing.

'Aye, no doubt some wee lassie will be bowled over by his flannel one day and there are a lot of unattached young lassies here tonight, but he better behave.' The song ended and Jimmy waved his wife over.

'Cathy, this is DCI Harry McNeil, and his better half, DS Alex Maxwell.'

'Hello, love,' she said smiling at Alex.

'Congratulations,' Harry said as Alex handed her the box.

'Thank you, sweetheart.' She looked at Harry. 'Jimmy's told me all about you, and I just want to say, I don't believe a word of it.' She laughed and patted his arm.

'Come on, you can sit at our table. I saved a space for you,' Dunbar said.

They were introduced to the others and drinks were brought for them. 'It's a free bar and her brother is picking up the tab. He's loaded and he's very generous so don't hold back.' He gave a waiter their order.

'Just a few sociable beers, Jimmy,' Harry said.

'A few sociable beers, he says. Did you hear that, Alex? You're a comedian, Harry.'

'I try. There's only two of us in Edinburgh and it's the other lad's day off.'

Jimmy chuckled as a waiter came across with the drinks.

'Look, there's the laddie now,' Jimmy said.

DS Robbie Evans walked off the dance floor with an older woman who was holding his hand tightly and obviously in no hurry to let it go. They made their way over.

'Oh, and who is this handsome young fella?' the woman said, discarding Evans for a moment.

'Harry, Alex, this is my sister-in-law, Rita. Rita, this is Harry McNeil and his girlfriend.'

Harry stood up and shook her hand. 'Nice to meet you, Rita.'

'Aw, you're spoken for, Harry?' Jimmy said there were some nice people coming through from Edinburgh and I thought my luck might have been in.' She laughed loudly.

'Rita is currently unattached. Looking for a new Mr Right.'

'I'm going to get a drink, Jimmy,' Rita said. 'Don't let young Robbie go anywhere. Nice meeting you folks.'

'One dance, you said,' Evans complained. 'Her hands were all over me.'

'It's called taking one for the team. If Rita's happy, then Cathy is happy, and it all trickles downhill. I knew you'd understand.' He grinned at Evans.

'I'm glad I didn't wear my lucky suit.'

'You should have brought your sister along. Pretended she was your girlfriend.'

'That's not even funny. Rita mentioned something about a thong, and I don't think she meant karaoke.' He looked pleadingly at Alex. 'Save me from certain death DS Maxwell; have a shuffle on the dance floor with me. If you don't mind, sir?' he said to Harry.

'Dance away, my friend.'

Alex laughed and Evans led her to the dance floor before Rita came back.

Jimmy sat next to Harry. 'You've got a bad one back home then, mate.'

'Aye. A young bloke stabbed on his doorstep. That's why I asked you to try and locate the wife's ex-husband. The victim was also married before but I have my team going over to Fife to talk to the victim's ex.'

'You said you thought this isn't a random killing?'

'It's an upscale part of town, Jimmy. Things like that don't happen. For some reason, he was targeted and we want to rule out all angles. The wife's ex is a soldier, or he was at one time. Did you manage to trace him?'

'Of course we did. I had my DI go and arrest him this afternoon.'

'Arrest him? We just want to talk to him.'

Jimmy grinned. 'You were in luck; we have an outstanding arrest warrant out for him. Failing to appear in court. And you'll never guess what for?'

'It wasn't murder.'

'I wish. He owed his missus back money for child support. The twat owes her thousands and he was due in court three months ago. He didn't turn up, changed his address and the ex couldn't find him. But we did.'

'Good work, Jimmy.'

'Of course it was. I had one of my confidentials drop his name and where we could go and pick him up. But the eejit made it easy for us. Now he's kicking his heels down in my cells.'

'At least we know he's not going anywhere now.'

'Just kick back and watch young Robbie trying to dodge my sister-in-law for the rest of the night.'

'I'll drink to that.'

TEN

Glasgow on a dull Sunday morning at the end of April was pretty much the same as Edinburgh at the end of April; dull and threatening to rain. Harry stood looking out of the hotel window down onto the River Clyde below, imagining what it must have looked like years before when they built ships here. A huge industrial crane stood on the dock, like it was waiting for something to do and nobody had told it to go home, that it had been made redundant.

Alex came up behind him and put her arms around him. He was wearing a robe over his shorts and T-shirt.

'Penny for them.' she said, as she moved beside him. She put an arm around him.

'I wonder what my dad would have thought of this place. I mean, it was revitalised when he was alive, of course, but I remember he and my mum came through to the SECC to see Debbie Harry a long time ago.

Things have changed even more since then. Like this hotel, for example. Things just spring up around you, the landscape changing forever.'

'Why the melancholy?' She smiled at him.

'I woke up and thought about my mum, and the promise I made to take my brother out for a pint. I mean, it's like being introduced to somebody who doesn't know how to have a chat. Somebody who you start telling your darkest secrets to just to make conversation.'

'It'll be fine, Harry.'

He turned to face her and put his arms around her. 'I know, but Derek is a pain in the arse. I never thought I'd say that about my little brother, but he made himself that way. Now my mother thinks the sun shines out of one of his orifices.'

Alex pulled back a little. 'If you don't want to go, then just tell your mother that you don't want to deal with Derek just now.'

'I would have, but—'

'But you want to hear more about his theory of why he thinks Bobby was murdered.'

'Am I that transparent?'

'Yes. And truth be told, I'm a bit curious myself.'

'You know he's just talking nonsense as usual, don't you?' Harry said.

'If he is, then just dismiss him. Don't get me wrong, I like your brother, but I don't like the way he acts. There's a difference.'

'I know. I'm the same, really.'

'So, make arrangements and have him come over to Edinburgh and have a pint with him.'

'I will.' He looked at his watch. 'You'd better go and have a shower. Jimmy's sending a patrol car and it will be here in half an hour.'

'Why don't *we* go and have a shower?'

He smiled at her. 'Just don't tell Jimmy we did this. He already thinks I take advantage of you.'

'You do take advantage of me.'

'Honey, I can't see any man taking advantage of you.' He let her take him by the hand.

'You two look like the Glasgow air is doing you a world of good,' Jimmy Dunbar said as Harry and Alex were shown into his office in Helen Street police station. 'I take it the hotel room is okay?'

'It's magic, thanks again, Jimmy,' Alex said.

'The manager is a friend of mine. He cut me a deal, so you won't have to put your hand in your pocket. I spoke to him yesterday, and the room is on me. And him, if he knows what's good for him.'

'There's no need for that,' Harry said.

'Nonsense. I said you could have stayed at our place but Cathy said you two lovebirds would be wanting your privacy. I don't know what she thought you were going to get up to. Chess, I said, but what do I know?'

'It's a nice room though. I appreciate it,' Harry said, his cheeks tinged with red.

'Aye, check mate.' He smiled at Harry.

The door to the incident room opened and Robbie Evans walked in. 'Sorry I'm late, sir,' he said through the open doorway of Dunbar's office.

'Don't apologise, son. How did your night go?'

'If you mean, did I take another one for the team and take Rita home, I have to say, sadly, no.'

'She was waiting outside for you last time I saw.'

'That's what hotel kitchens are for; slipping out unnoticed. I shared a taxi with DCI McNeil and DS Maxwell. I just wanted to make sure the taxi driver didn't take them the long way round to their hotel.'

'Sure you did. And there I was, standing outside, consoling Rita, who was convinced you were trying to dodge her. Crying her eyes out, she was.'

'You're kidding.'

'Of course I am, ya wee eejit. She went home with one of the band members.'

'Which one? The clarinet player?'

'Anyway,' Dunbar said, standing up from the other side of his desk, 'let's go and talk to Michelle Naismith's ex. He's an ex-squaddie but don't worry, I've got a couple of boys in there with him who were in the marines. If it kicks off, we'll get a definitive answer on who's better, army or navy. Let's go. Alex, Robbie;

you can observe through the mirror.' He picked up a buff folder from his desk.

He led them out into the corridor and they went down one level to where there were interrogation rooms. Alex and Robbie went into the little observation room next to the interrogation room that Harry and Dunbar entered.

Trevor Avery sat at the table and looked round when the two detectives arrived. The big uniforms stood to one side, looking disappointed that they hadn't had the chance to restrain the army bloke.

Avery was a big guy and looked like he worked out. His hair was unkempt and he had stubble on his face.

'Wait outside,' Dunbar said to one of them, and the man left. The other one stayed.

The detectives sat down, Dunbar putting the folder on the table and Harry looked at the man having had the chance to read the bio that Dunbar's DI had emailed to his laptop and which he had perused over a coffee earlier.

'What is this bollocks?' Avery said after Dunbar had started the tape rolling. A camera above them was recording everything. 'Arresting me on some triviality?'

'It's hardly trivial, your kid not getting food and clothes,' Dunbar said.

'He's sixteen. What clothes does he need?'

'He's sixteen, and when my son was sixteen, he was always ripping his jeans and getting his shirts dirty. God knows, he needed new shoes every few months.'

Dunbar looked him in the eye. 'I'm sure your son is the same.'

'Look, he doesn't want for anything. He gets all the clothes he needs and wants. I tried to give her money, but I lost my job and Michelle knew that. I told her that I would catch up with the payments, but she didn't want to listen. So she got some arsewipe solicitor to hound me.'

'That why you didn't turn up for your court appearance?' Harry said.

'Exactly. It's not like I was raking it in and didn't want to give her money. You can check everything. It's all a matter of record. My unemployment record. She's just being a bitch.'

'She's just being mamma bear, looking out for her son.'

'Her new husband's loaded.'

'Her new husband's dead,' Dunbar said.

'What?' Avery sat forward. 'Dead? What happened?'

'You mean to say you don't know?' Harry said.

'Naw, I don't know anything.'

'He was stabbed to death on his doorstep.' Harry let the words sink in then he watched Avery's face change.

'Aw, wait a minute; you're trying to pin this on me?'

'Nobody's trying to pin anything on anybody,' Dunbar said. 'We need to ask you a few questions to eliminate you, that's all. You *do* want to be eliminated, don't you?'

'Of course I do. Why would I want to go down for murdering that lowlife when it wasn't me?'

'Help us help you, Trevor,' Harry said.

Avery shook his head. 'Why would I want to kill him? We didn't see eye-to-eye, but you lot knew that already. I've never pretended to like him. And why should I? She was seeing him before we'd even split up, although I can't prove that. Officially, they met after we separated. After two years, we divorced and Michelle married him. Then they had the kid. The one who died.'

Harry looked puzzled. 'Michelle didn't mention that. Can you tell us more?'

'It wasn't anything criminal, like. The bairn had a defective heart. They said she would have to get surgery when she was a bit older, but her heart couldn't take the strain or something. She wasn't my daughter, but it was hard just the same. Dennis was just a wee boy at the time and he was confused and upset.'

'Did you get him help?' Dunbar said.

'Aye, we did. Michelle got grief counselling and she took Dennis to see some bloke. He started misbehaving and she was all softly-softly with him.'

'Whereas you would have given him a beltin', eh?'

Avery made a face. 'No' exactly. I was in the Paras, but it's bad patter to hit a wee laddie, especially my own son. Naw, I didn't lift a hand to him, and I told him, if stepdaddy ever hit him, he was to tell me and Clark wouldn't do it again.'

'Is that what happened here?' Harry said. 'Clark hit Dennis and you sorted him out?'

'I told you, I didn't hit the weasel. You think I'd stab him on his doorstep and never see my son again after you lot banged me up? Give me a break. I would have run the bastard over.'

'Good to know, for future reference,' Dunbar said.

'I didn't touch him. But maybe you should ask Arthur Daniels. Maybe he would know something.'

'Who's this?' Harry asked.

'The owner of the escort agency that Michelle worked for. Not many people knew about that, but she used to escort old farts to functions and the like. She swore she never slept with any of them, and I believe it was up to each individual, but if they wanted to make extra, they would go the whole way.'

'Where can we find this Daniels?'

'Edinburgh. He's not a big player, and he supplies decent-looking birds for old codgers who have more money than sense. She got to go to the theatre and the like, on the arm of some gin-tottering old bastard and to other places where the guy wanted a bit of eye candy on his arm. Michelle scrubs up pretty well.' He stared off into the large mirror behind Harry and Dunbar. 'Truth be told, I was always proud to be out and about with her.'

'What happened to your marriage?' Harry asked.

'I got jealous. The escorting thing got to me. She never stayed out overnight, nothing like that, and as I said, she promised she didn't sleep with them. It was just so the older blokes could show face, you know, not turn up to some do looking like a sad sack who can't get a woman. Some of them only wanted her services now and again, when they were going to the opera or some such shite. Others when they were going to a party, stuff like that. I'm sure there are plenty of seedy escort agencies where the women are glorified prozzies, but this wasn't like that. But there was one guy who gave her a bit of grief.'

'What sort of grief?' Harry asked.

'One bloke she went out with. It was to some function in Edinburgh. He sent a car for her, she went with him to this function, and he was supposed to send her back in a car. She would get picked up at Arthur Daniels' office. He would be there, or one of the guys he hired for security, so they were never alone there. This guy, I can't remember his name, said he wanted to take her back to his place, thinking she was a high-priced hooker, and she refused. He told her that nobody refused him anything and she would be sorry. Then dead flowers would be delivered to our house. He'd obviously found out where we lived. I wanted to sort the bastard, but she refused to tell me who it was. Then I caught some young guy delivering the flowers but he was a delivery driver for the flower shop. I couldn't get any details but after that, it stopped. I think he must have moved on to somebody else.'

Harry made a note to find out the details from Arthur Daniels.

'How was Michelle and Clark's marriage, would you say?' Dunbar asked.

Avery shrugged. 'Like yours, I suppose; you argue sometimes, but then you get past it and move on. That's what Dennis tells me.'

'Did Dennis ever express an interest in moving back in with you?' Harry asked.

Avery gave a small laugh. 'All the time. But I told him to wait until he was sixteen and then we'd talk about it. Not that he didn't like Clark, but he wanted to be with his dad. Now he's sixteen and wants to come live with me after he finishes school.'

'Boy's usually want to be with their mum, in my experience,' Harry said, and he briefly thought about his own brother.

'He did at first, but considering Michelle was his stepmother at first, I thought it was only right he should come and live with me.'

'Wait a minute,' Dunbar said. 'You said that Clark Naismith was Dennis's stepfather, so that would mean Michelle is his mother.'

'Technically. You see, when I first met Michelle, I was a widower. Dennis was only a year old and Michelle and I got married six months after we met. She fell into the role of mother and wanted to be his mother for the rest of his life, and so she adopted him. Legally, she's his mother but not his birth mother.'

'And she wanted to keep him when you split up.'

'Aye. She said a boy needs a mother. Besides, her solicitor made sure Dennis stayed with her and since my son didn't remember his own mother, Michelle got to keep him. And that's what pisses me off; I paid my dues for my boy. She knew I was out of work and I promised to send her money when I got on my feet, including back money, but she got wind of the fact that Dennis wants to come and live with me, so she wanted to make sure that didn't happen. That's why she sent you lot after me.'

'Where were you on Friday evening?' Harry asked.

'Down at the social with some of my mates. I got a job a couple of weeks ago and I was finally to get out for a pint again. I was with my pals all night.'

'We'll need names and numbers,' Dunbar said, sliding a pen and paper across the table.

Avery wrote the names down.

'Where were you staying when you were out of work?' Harry asked.

'At my ma's place. I'm originally from here but Michelle's from Edinburgh that's why we lived through there but when we divorced, I came back here. I couldn't afford to stay in Edinburgh.'

'What job do you have now?' Dunbar asked.

'I'm a roofer. I start next week. It's hard work but it pays well. I'm doing it for my boy.'

Dunbar looked at Harry who nodded. They wrapped the interview up and Avery was taken back to the cells.

'The procurator fiscal will release him tomorrow, no doubt. He'll have to appear in court but I'm sure they won't be that harsh on him if he gives Michelle the cash.'

'I'm surprised the child support agency didn't catch up with him,' Harry said as they left the room.

'Nobody knew he was at his mother's, but Avery bought a little runabout car and that was registered to his mother's address.' He stopped at the door to the viewing room. 'What do you think? He your guy?'

'I'm not sure, Jimmy; he's a trained killer who used to jump out of aeroplanes for a living and I'm sure he could have killed Naismith without breaking sweat, but I think he's more looking forward to having his son move through with him than angry at the ex's husband so why would he risk it?'

'Could be a smoke screen,' Robbie Evans said as he and Alex came out of the observation room.

'Gut instinct says not, but we're not ruling him out.'

'I'll have my DI run down those names. I'll let you know what we find,' Dunbar said.

'I found an address for Arthur Daniels,' Alex said.

'That quick?' Harry said.

'I googled him.'

'Maybe we should ask Google if Avery murdered

Clark Naismith. They know the answer to everything else.'

'Come on, let's go and get some lunch before you head back east,' Dunbar said. 'Cathy's doing a nice roast.'

'That sounds great,' Harry said.

'I haven't had a roast in ages,' Alex said. 'Maybe Cathy can give me some tips on how to cook one.'

'I'm sure she would love to. You're invited too, Robbie.'

'Oh, cheers, boss.'

Alex and Robbie walked in front along the corridor.

'I'm not going to tell Robbie that Rita is going to be there too. It might scare him.'

'I can't wait to see his face.'

ELEVEN

The house was a large semi-detached near the end of Dewar Street in Dunfermline. A light wind blew in from the field across the road as DI Ronnie Vallance stepped out of the passenger side of the car and stretched.

'One too many last night, sir?' DS Eve Bell said.

'I wish. Babysitting our little granddaughter. My daughter's first one. She's great but got up in the middle of the night for a pee. Then she wanted a story told to her.'

'The joys of being a grandpa, eh?' She smiled at him. 'But you wouldn't have it any other way.'

'I certainly would not. I have twin sixteen-year-old sons too, but there's plenty of time for them to populate the planet.'

It was sunny, bathing the old stone house in a bright light. The blue door opened as they walked up the pathway. A woman who looked to be in her forties was standing waiting for them to approach. If this was the first Mrs Naismith, Vallance knew her age to be thirty-eight.

'Mrs Naismith?' Vallance asked. 'Or formerly Naismith, I should say.'

'Ms Leslie now. Dawn. Please come in.' She stood back and let the two detectives walk past her into a quiet hallway. No sound of a TV, no children running about. The smell of polish was thick in the air.

'Through to the right,' Dawn instructed.

The living room was a fair size. No TV, Vallance saw, thinking this must be the formal room where the minister was invited in for tea, or where the bridge club met. Dawn Leslie gave off the same vibe a woman in her sixties might, and he expected two cats to make an appearance any moment.

'Take a seat,' she said as the detectives stood in the middle of the room like they were expecting a game of musical chairs to break out at any moment. Vallance took an overstuffed armchair while Eve sat on a settee to the side of him. Dawn chose a chair next to an unused fireplace housing a vase with long grass in it instead of coal.

'Thank you for seeing us today,' Vallance said, 'and sorry for your loss.'

'It's not my loss, Inspector. It's *her* loss. When you told me on the phone what happened, I was shocked, but not sad. He's my ex-husband. He left me for her, and although he died in a horrific way, you can't expect me to feel sorry for him.'

'We'd just like to ask you a few questions,' Eve said in a soothing voice. She had worked with Vallance years before and knew he wasn't one for suffering fools gladly, and sometimes the lines were blurred.

'Okay. I've watched enough TV shows to know that I'm a suspect. *Woman kills ex-husband in jealous rage*. It didn't happen. If I was going to kill him it would have been a long time ago when I was angry with him. Now, I live my own life.'

'Did you remarry?' Vallance asked.

'No. I have a boyfriend now, although at my age, *boyfriend* makes it sound like I'm going out with a sixteen-year-old. I went back to using my maiden name. Joe and I are dating, but we don't live with each other. We've been seeing each other for going on seven years now and we're happy with the way things are going.'

'What does Joe do for a living?' Eve asked.

'He's a bank manager with Scottish National. Although God knows the number of branches they're shutting down isn't funny. Online shopping killed the high street branches. Joe moved into the head office over at Gogarburn.'

'Where Clark worked,' Vallance said.

'There are jigsaw pieces, Inspector, but unless they're all from the same puzzle, they won't make up the correct picture. Yes, Joe and Clark worked for the same bank in the same building but they didn't work in the same department. Did they know of each other? I would be a fool to lie to you and say no, because you're going to check, so yes, they did know of each other. But there was never any animosity between them. Why should there be? Joe isn't the violent type. And Clark was the one who left me and I'm happy now.'

'How was Clark as a husband? Like, was he a jolly guy, or did he have a temper?' Eve asked.

'Clark go fighting?' She gave a small humourless laugh. 'No. As the saying goes, he was the very epitome of being a lover not a fighter. That was the whole problem at the end of the day; he loved women. Being with them, being around them. I'm surprised our marriage lasted as long as it did. But I caught him cheating on me and that was the end of the road.'

'Do you think he might have cheated on Michelle?'

Dawn shrugged. 'A leopard and its spots are not easily parted. Why would you think he would change his lousy ways just because he was married to Michelle? You have to understand what Clark was like; it was the hunt for him. He liked the chase. That was all part of the game. When he was finished, he was like the big game cat; he feasted and then walked away from the carcass because the carcass didn't provide any fun for him anymore. If I was to hazard a guess, I'd say he has had multiple affairs in the time he's been with her. He can't help himself. It's a compulsion.' She looked at them. '*Couldn't* help himself.'

'He was a family man, though,' Eve said, thinking about her own husband and daughter. 'Sometimes bringing a life into this world makes a difference.'

'I agree,' Dawn said, 'but not all the time. Sometimes a man is just an animal. I think Clark was like this. He was a good-looking man, and he knew it. *God's gift* they call it, don't they? Clark was handsome, but he was lacking in the intelligence department.'

'And yet he was a bank manager,' Vallance said.

'How do you think he got up the career ladder so fast? It wasn't because of his intellectual skills, I can assure you. I work for the bank as well. I started there before he did, but I had a university degree in business. I met Clark, who was basically a ditch-digger. Sure, he could charm anybody, and he had a smile to die for, but he could hardly string a sentence together. By God, he couldn't even write a bloody letter to apply for a job. I had to do that for him. I'm the one who put in a word for him at the bank. And he charmed his way into the manager's position. Luckily for him, he and his boss both supported the same football team. They became friends out of work, and the boss put in a word for him. Clark couldn't have climbed the ladder on his own merit.'

'Still, he must have been able to do his job,' Eve said.

'Oh, yes, but with practice, even a monkey can tie his own shoelaces. When he was manager, he had people working under him. If he was stuck on anything, he could always ask the underlings. It was how he sailed through life.'

'I know this is a personal question, but you said Clark cheated on you. Was it with Michelle?'

Dawn hesitated for a moment before answering. 'Yes. She worked in the bank as well. We were at a co-worker's fortieth birthday party at a golf club. It was a great night; the drink was flowing and everybody was having a good time on the dance floor. Except Clark, who was outside with Michelle, having a good time. It was shortly after that they got together. They had a baby who died.'

'Oh God,' Eve said. 'That's sad.'

'It was. I felt for him, I really did. He would come round here and we would talk, he'd get drunk and pass out. Michelle and I had some fights over that, but he did convince her that nothing had gone on, which it hadn't. Months later, he stopped coming round. I don't know if it was the grief dissipating or if Michelle had told him he needed to stop. But I was here for him.'

Vallance sat further back into the chair. 'You've told us that Clark couldn't stop messing around with other women, and we now know that included married women. Did he ever get any threats from the husbands of those women?'

'There was one guy who said he was going to kick Clark's head in, but as far as I know, nothing came of that. It was an angry drunken phone call with a message left on our answering machine. I certainly know that Clark didn't ever look like he'd been in a fight. There might have been other threats, but if there were, he didn't tell me. That would mean admitting he was seeing other women.'

'You knew about them,' Eve said.

'Yes. I knew before the message on the machine. I didn't want to believe it, at first, but then I knew for sure. I confronted him and he promised me it would stop, but it didn't.'

'Did he confide in you about anything else?' Vallance asked. 'Like he confided in you when the baby died?'

'Sometimes we would meet in the cafeteria. This was after Michelle had the other baby and she left the bank. Clark and I would talk sometimes. It was like I was a friend to him, somebody he could talk to about his little infidelities. I should have told him to sod off, but I think deep down I was pleased when he was telling me that he was skating on thin ice.'

'Anything recently?'

'Yes. There was one woman he had been chasing for ages. They would sit and laugh in the cafeteria, and anybody with decent eyesight could see they were fooling around. The husband called up one day looking for him. That was weeks ago. I don't know what the outcome was, but he didn't turn up to work with a black eye or anything.'

'And he didn't elaborate about that?'

'No. We would only sit and talk at lunch when he

was between women. Or if he thought a relationship was going down the tubes.'

'When was the last time you saw him?' Eve asked.

'At work, on Friday, when he asked me to come along to the pub afterwards. We would go to Corstorphine. A small group of us. He was slowly getting hammered. He told me he wanted to have a word with me about something. I thought he was just wanting to spout off about another conquest of his, but he seemed different this time. He told me he wanted to tell me something. But then his friends were roughhousing and he forgot. I reminded him before we all started leaving and he said he would call me this weekend.'

'And you have no clue what this was going to be about?'

'No. I don't know if he was in trouble this time or not. But we'll never know.'

'Do you know who he left the pub with?'

'Two of his friends from the department. I'll give you their names. I left after them and got a train from Gogar. Joe picked me up from the station. He was working from home that day. He does a bit of travelling with the bank and he ends up working from home sometimes.'

Vallance stood up as Dawn left the room and she came back with a piece of paper with a couple of names written on it. 'I only know them from work. I don't know their address or phone numbers. Sorry.'

'Don't worry. You've been most helpful. We'll be following up with these people at the bank tomorrow.'

Outside, the wind had died down and it felt warmer. 'What do you reckon?' Vallance said.

'I think our Clarkie boy put it around, and maybe one of the husbands took offence,' Eve replied.

'That's certainly one avenue we have to explore. Maybe he got into it with somebody in the pub and they followed him home. Just because his missus says he didn't like to fight, doesn't mean to say she knew him. I worked with a bloke who was nice as ninepence until he had a few whiskies then he would take your head off. And he wouldn't remember doing it afterwards. Let's find out if Clark was a secret boxer.'

TWELVE

'What's on your mind?' Alex asked as they headed back to Edinburgh on the M8.

'What, do you mean am I wondering why the car is having trouble getting off the ground or did I remember to pack a sick bag?'

'Ha ha. Very funny. I'm barely speeding. This car just flies along so nicely.'

'*Flies* being the operative word. Why don't you slow it down a notch?'

'My grandmother drives faster than this.'

'You told me she was in a nursing home.'

'And?' She laughed. 'That's what you get when you buy an Audi instead of cadging an old beater off the pool manager. A car that can actually keep up with the other traffic.'

'I just want to get home in one piece.'

She took a hand off the wheel and patted his leg. 'Aw, don't worry, I'll make sure Harry gets home safe.'

'Both hands on the wheel. I swear to God, my life started to flash before my eyes. I don't know about you but seeing your sixteen-year-old self back at the school leavers dance is not a pretty sight. Not something I wanted to re-experience.'

She laughed. 'I had fun at my school-leavers.'

'I got drunk and puked in the school car park. In front of my date.'

'Oh, everlasting love, was it?' She laughed and put both hands back on the wheel. 'It wasn't Vanessa, was it?'

'No, it bloody well wasn't.'

Alex pulled into the fast lane and put her foot down, overtaking a slower moving truck, then pulled back in front of it, slowing down.

'Obviously a Spitfire pilot in another life,' Harry said, checking his watch and realising more parac-etamol was still another couple of hours away.

'Jimmy and Cathy are a nice couple,' Alex said, staring ahead out of the windscreen.

'They are. And their kids are nice too. Although hardly kids anymore.'

'Once you're a parent, they're always your kids.'

'True. Chance will always be my wee boy. Although he's seventeen next month.'

'Maybe he'll want to come and live with us one day.'

'I'd love that.' Harry thought about his son for a little while, about how he lived with his mother and grandmother now. Harry was sure his ex-mother-in-law was a witch and had voiced this opinion to her on many an occasion.

'Have you thought about having more kids?' Alex asked.

'If the right person came along.'

'What do you mean by that?' Her smile dropped.

'Oh, I mean I had thought about it before you came into my life. I never thought I'd meet anybody again, that I was going to spend my twilight years fading away into a bottle. Then I met you.'

'You know, Jimmy's anniversary got me thinking. About life, love and how sometimes a chance for something comes into your life and you let it slip through your fingers.' She turned to him and smiled again. 'That's why I wasn't going to let you slip through my fingers. I fell for you, Harry McNeil, and I am going to be the best girlfriend you've ever had. And before you ask, yes, I *can* see myself being Mrs McNeil. I know we're going to sign the final papers so the flat is ours, and I know there's no such thing as a guaranteed relationship, but I am giving it a hundred per cent.'

'I know you are, and so am I. To answer your question, yes, I can see myself being a dad again. But I'm forty-one this year.'

'I'm turning thirty-one this year, so if we are

thinking about it, I don't want to think about it too long.'

'I agree.'

Alex slowed down on the approach to the Edinburgh bypass and swung up onto it, heading for the Gogar roundabout.

'Please don't laugh when I say this, but I'm sort of old-fashioned. Well, not too old-fashioned because I'm living with you, but whenever I thought about having kids, I was already married, in my scenario.' She slowed down on the approach to the roundabout as the traffic lights turned green and the traffic began to move. 'I would like to be married when I have kids. I want to have a solid marriage just like my folks have.'

Harry nodded. He agreed with her sentiments, but he knew from experience that being married with a child didn't guarantee a perfect relationship. Especially when one of you stops trying.

He smiled at her, not wanting to shoot her down in flames. 'I agree. I feel differently about you than I felt with Morag. It's different this time round. But let's get the deeds signed and then we'll go to the next level.'

'We've already reached the next level,' she said laughing.

'Yer a wicked wee lassie right enough. My mother warned me about you leading me astray.'

'Yeah, right. There was no leading, matey.'

Harry's phone rang as Alex shot the car up past the casino on Maybury Road. He groaned as he read the name on the screen. 'What the bloody hell does he want now?'

'Derek, I assume.'

He looked over at Alex. 'I think so. It's not his name so he's probably using somebody else's so I won't know it's him until I pick up.' The phone sat in his lap unanswered.

'You should really talk to him,' Alex said.

'I already told my mother I'd have a drink with him. I wish he would just wait until I call him.'

'I think he's anxious to reconnect with you.'

'That and to tell me where Lord Lucan went to live.' He pressed the answer button. 'Derek.'

'Is this DCI McNeil, Edinburgh Division?'

'Who am I speaking to?' Harry said, looking across at Alex.

'This is DI Matt Keen, sir. Fife Division.'

'I'm DCI McNeil.'

'You have a brother, Derek McNeil?'

'I do. What's he done now?'

'He was attacked last night, sir. He's in Dunfermline Royal. I'm at the hospital right now.'

'Jesus. Is he okay?'

'He's been in overnight.'

'Is my mother there?'

'There's nobody here. We found him in his house in Dalgety Bay. He was the only one there. There's no sign of your mother, sir.'

THIRTEEN

Keen was waiting for them outside Derek's room. He was a tall, skinny man dressed in a suit that needed pressing.

'One of my officers tried calling you earlier, sir,' he said to Harry, as if he was going to get a strip torn off him.

'It's fine. Is my mother okay?'

'She's fine. She turned up when the uniforms were there. She had been at a friend's house. Luckily she wasn't home when it went down.'

'Thank God,' Alex said.

'I saw someone had tried calling my phone and I thought it was somebody trying to sell me timeshare or something. Tell me what happened.' Alex was standing next to him.

'We got a call last night about a disturbance at a house

in Dalgety Bay. Local uniform turned up and found the front door open and the house trashed. Your brother was lying unconscious on the floor. One of the neighbours told us who he was. She also had a couple of emergency contact numbers but none of them were answered.'

'You get anybody for it?' Alex asked.

'No. Neighbours saw a red hatchback leaving the street at high speed. It's a dead-end street so we're hoping somebody might have seen something, but despite us having uniforms talking to neighbours today, there hasn't been anything reported.'

A doctor approached them. 'Mr McNeil?'

'Yes, that's me. How's he doing?'

'He's badly shaken and bruised a bit, but nothing serious. No broken bones. No concussion either, despite him being struck on the back of the head.'

'Can I go in and see him?'

'Yes, you can go in now.'

'I'll wait here,' Keen said.

'I'll wait here too,' Alex said. 'Maybe this is a talk you need to have privately.'

Harry put a hand on her arm before he opened the door to the room and walked in.

Derek was lying in the bed with a machine hooked up to him, displaying his blood pressure and other vital signs.

'Harry! What are you doing here?'

Harry had thought the same thing himself as he

had stood in the corridor. The fact that Derek was flesh and blood didn't have any weight to it.

'Oh, you know, I was just passing and I thought I'd pop in. Maybe have a coffee, that sort of thing.' He shook his head.' What the hell do you think I'm doing here?'

'You might not have noticed, but I'm feeling a little bit under the weather.'

Suddenly, Harry felt ashamed. Maybe it was time to give his brother a chance to explain. He sat down on one of the chairs. 'Tell me what happened.'

Derek looked past him at the wall, as if the TV was there, playing a re-run of what happened the day before.

'There were two of them. I was sitting in the living room watching TV when I heard the front door open. I thought it was Mum coming back in. Next thing I know, two blokes were running up the stairs and one of them smacked me.'

'Who were they? Did you recognise them?'

'They had masks on. One of them belted me good and proper and hit me over the head with something and down I went. The other one went... well, I don't know. I saw him leave the living room and that's all I remember.'

'What did they take?'

'I don't know. I spoke to mum earlier and she didn't say. She went back home and she's going through the house with a police officer.' He looked like he was going to break down for a moment. 'Christ, Harry, they could have killed me. They were ruthless bastards.'

'The Fife division think it was just a home invasion. Do you know any different?'

'*Just*? We could have been killed. And no, I don't know any different. But thinking and knowing are two different things, aren't they?'

'What do you mean?' Harry was starting to feel the heat in the room and opened another button on his shirt. He knew exactly what Derek meant.

'Come on, you're the detective, Harry; I already told you I think Bobby was murdered.'

'So you keep saying. But you haven't told me why you think this.'

'You haven't given me a chance.'

'The floor's all yours.'

Derek took a deep breath and let it out slowly before speaking. 'I noticed things, in the house. Not long after Bobby disappeared. Like things had been moved and not been put back properly. I started to think we had a poltergeist or something, but one day, I had been out and Mum was off to God knows where, and when I came back, I went into the kitchen and there it was, a partial footprint in the kitchen. It wasn't from me.'

'Did you mention this to Mum?'

'No. I mopped it up. I didn't want to worry her.'

'Don't you think it might have been a good idea to

tell her somebody was creeping about in her house when she wasn't there?'

'In hindsight, yes, but not at the time.'

'If somebody was coming into the house, how do you think they were getting in?'

'With a key. I thought that maybe somebody had murdered Bobby and taken his keys.'

'Again with the murder theory. He disappeared and was found washed up on the shore. He'd been in the water a long time, Derek.'

'You're a copper. It's your job to think suspiciously.'

'The pathologist's report said accidental death. He had a fractured skull, but it was consistent with falling onto rocks then into the water.'

'Somebody could have tossed him in there.'

'I work with facts, not suspicions or conspiracy theories.'

'It's just that I overheard him talking on the phone. I couldn't make out the conversation, but it was heated. Bobby ended the call by telling the other person it could all go away.'

'What was *it*?'

'I have no idea. But you know how he always had many irons in the fire. Maybe it was a shady deal. Who knows? But there was the time a few days before he disappeared that a guy came to the door to talk to him and he stepped out onto the doorstep. Bobby was angry with him.'

'Do you know who it was?'

Derek hesitated for a moment. 'Aye. Bobby called him by his name; it was Clark. Bobby opened the door again and I heard him tell this Clark guy that he was never to come to the house again. Then Clark told Bobby that he would be sorry.'

'Did you see this guy Clark's face?' Harry asked.

'Aye. It was the bloke who was murdered last Friday. Clark Naismith.'

FOURTEEN

'Guess who's invited out for dinner next weekend?' Alex said, pouring herself another cup of coffee.

'You know a question like that opens you up to all sorts of answers except an appropriate one.'

'Like?'

'Sorry, this is a trap and I won't walk into it.'

'Good catch there.' Suddenly she put on a serious face. 'Were you thinking about marriage because we were at Jimmy's do?'

'I wouldn't be buying this place with you if I didn't think marriage was on the cards. I know it is for you.'

'You think so?'

'Hey, come on, who could resist this?' He held his arms out sideways.

'I would like to be wined and dined before you get on one knee.'

He put his arms around her waist. 'Seriously, yes, I

would like to be your husband one day, and not in the far-off future either. I told you I'm in love with you, Alex Maxwell, and I meant it.'

'I love you too, Harry McNeil.'

He kissed her lightly then pulled back. 'I hope your mum and dad approve of me when we meet them on Saturday.'

Her eyes widened for a moment. 'How do you do that? Kiss me and know what I was going to talk to you about?'

'Easy; your mum called me while you were in the shower. Told me to remind you about Saturday. She sounds nice.'

'Don't let that fool you. They'll both be interrogating you, but in a subtle way.'

'Maybe I should wear my tinfoil helmet. That's always a conversation starter.'

'With a judge, maybe. But get a move on. We're going to the bank to speak with Clark Naismith's colleagues, remember?'

'I hadn't forgotten.'

'Whose car are we taking?'

Yours. I don't feel like driving.' Harry finished his own coffee.

'You mean Mad Mike the Mondeo is acting up again?'

'Define *acting up*?'

'He needs to go on one last journey. To the big scrapyard in the sky.'

'He's like me; needs a little attention now and again. We're both a bit mature.'

'You both like a little too much to drink, you mean.'

'If you say we're both over the hill, I will not spare the rod, Miss Maxwell.'

'That's another thing you and your car have in common; you don't run very well.'

'I swear to God, if you say we both leak, *I'll* be driving that little red hairdresser's car you have. Really put it through its paces.'

'She. And yeah, right. I have my seat fixed perfectly. Last time you drove, it took me two days to get the rear-view mirror back to its original position.'

'First world problems, eh? You'll have to let me drive your Audi if Mike finally decides enough is enough.'

'Bloody cheapskate. I told you to buy another Honda...'

The Scottish National bank's world headquarters were out at Gogarburn, built on the site of an old asylum. It was a modern edifice, opposite Edinburgh airport.

'Some people think that the loonies didn't leave,' a young man said as he walked Harry and Alex along a corridor. Harry thought that HR would be putting in for overtime the amount of paperwork they'd have to fill out after the man's comment. *Loony* wasn't PC anymore, and Harry wondered when the transition had taken place. But as things went, loony wasn't in the top ten most offensive things you could call a person nowadays.

'Did you know Clark Naismith well?' Alex asked. A quick phone call to HR had given them a heads-up that they would be wanting to speak with members of Naismith's team, the staff who worked under him in his section. Which consisted of five people, including Malcolm *Call me Malc* Weston who was now their tour guide.

'Don't you wonder where they all went?' he asked, stopping outside an office. 'When they closed the asylum.'

'The hardcore patients were transferred to Carstairs, if memory serves me correctly. Others were put into the care of the community,' Harry said, and it was all he could do to stop himself from calling the man an ignorant bastard.

'I still say they should have built this place on a brown site, further up the road. There are plenty of people who would have gotten their pockets lined on that one.' He knocked on the door and they heard a person shouting from behind it, instructing them to come in.

Their guide opened it and spoke to the person sitting behind the desk, and stood to one side to let the detectives enter.

'Come in, please,' the woman said. 'Take a seat.'

Harry felt like he was at the bank for a job interview as he and Alex took seats opposite her.

'Martha Mays, head of HR.' She sat back in her chair, like the headmistress who'd brought them in for a dressing-down.

'We're here about Clark Naismith,' he said.

'I know.' It was said in a condescending tone, like Harry should have known she already knew.

'We're doing some background on him,' Alex said, noting the woman hadn't shown any remorse.

'Normally, I'd be gutted if any member of the bank had been taken in this way, but I'm sure there's a special place in hell reserved for him.'

'Why do you say that?' Harry asked.

'You mean his wife didn't tell you what he was like?' She gave a smile, full of menace.

'Why don't you give us your version?'

Martha leaned forward and picked up a pen from her desk. She tapped it a few times on the top, as if she was the drummer in a band and was giving the cue to the other members. *One, two, three.*

'He was a complete bastard. Here in HR, it's our job to give advice and support to anybody who is experiencing a problem, and Clark caused some problems.'

'In what way?'

Again with the tapping, which was starting to get on Harry's nerves, but he ignored it.

'He was, as the Americans like to say, *a player*. He fooled around on his wife all the time. We got wind of it, but it wasn't really a sackable offense, even if we didn't like it. He was skating on thin ice though. Him and his cronies. You know what they call themselves?'

She looked at them both as if she expected them to know, or at the very least, hazard a guess. Harry could guess what they called Martha, but more than likely only behind her back.

He shook his head, her cue to let them in on it.

'*The Fireball Club*. They call themselves that because each of them together make a fireball. They've elevated themselves up to God status. They're all married, but they all go out drinking together after work, and each of them thinks they were put on this earth to please women. To be honest, I thought that sort of behaviour had been relegated to the eighties, but it's alive and well in the twenty-first century.'

'Who are we talking about here? You got some names?'

'I can give you names, Chief Inspector, but only in the context that you want to speak to them as Naismith's friends and colleagues. Their behaviour doesn't bring the bank's reputation into disrepute, more's the pity, so my hands are tied, but it doesn't stop them from being pigs. One person you should talk to is a young woman called Sasha Young. She was on the wrong end of the *Fireballs* apparently, but it was outside bank hours, so again, my hands were tied.'

'Where can we find her?'

'She's on sick leave. I can get her details for you.'

'Thank you. Did Mr Naismith ever get into trouble here?' Alex asked.

'No. I hate to admit it, but his work was sterling. His team members spoke highly of him. His only fault was, he couldn't stay loyal to his wife.'

'Did anybody have a problem with him?'

'Not that I know of. And no official channels were gone through if they did. Nobody lodged an official complaint.'

'We'd also like to talk to Tommy Gallagher. Can somebody go fetch him?'

'Certainly. The break room will be empty just now. Or it should be. You can use that to talk to Mr Gallagher.' She picked up her phone and spoke into it. 'Malcolm's away to get him now.'

'If you can think of anything else, please contact us,' Harry said, standing up and taking a business card out of his wallet and handing it to her.

Outside in the corridor, they waited. Through the open doorway, they could see a large open-plan office with people sitting at desks.

'I'd be bored out my crust working in here,' Harry said.

'Me too. I never fancied office work. My dad worked in an office all of his life and he loved it, but it wasn't for me.'

A few minutes later, *Call me Malc* came towards them with another man in tow. 'This is Tommy Gallagher,' he said, making the introductions.

'Thanks, Malcolm,' Gallagher said.

'It's Malc, ya bastard,' Malc said in a low voice as he walked away.

Gallagher made a face, shrugged his shoulders and laughed a little. 'Calling him Malcolm all the time winds the bastard up. He works in HR and thinks he owns the place. He wants everybody to call him Malc. You should see what they write about him on the toilet wall. And it isn't *Malc was here.*'

'Not a popular bloke, then?' Harry said.

'You could say that.'

'Can we talk in the break room, Mr Gallagher?' Alex asked.

'We could, but I would prefer it if we talked outside in the car park.'

They followed him downstairs and past the security desk. Outside, it was windy, snatching Gallagher's cigarette smoke away after he lit it. 'Walls have ears. Windows have eyes. Don't look now, but Martha Mays is standing looking out of her window at us.'

Harry looked up.

'I said, don't look now. There was no ambiguity in that.'

'I'm a detective. Sometimes I want to see for myself.'

Gallagher took another puff. 'The whole property is a no-smoking zone now. Times used to be where they would have a smoking room, according to the old-timers.'

'How about Clark Naismith? What can you tell us about him?' Harry said, bringing his gaze back to ground zero.

'Clark liked to party. By God, he liked the women too. Don't get me wrong, I thought he was daft, messing around on his wife, but we had such a good time when we were out. We fed off each other. I'd set up a gag, he'd knock it out the park, and vice versa. We were a good team with the women, and they enjoyed it. But we never lied to them. They knew what it was all about, and they were there for a good time too.'

Harry could see Alex's face cloud over for a moment. Memories of her own ex-fiancé cheating on her no doubt shooting through her mind.

'Is that what went down last Friday before he was murdered?' she asked.

Gallagher looked at her. 'No. Last Friday was just a few pints in Corstorphine before we headed our own way. I wanted to go home and get changed, but Clarkie said he had to go home as his missus was going out somewhere.'

'You two didn't have a conflict in the pub with anybody?' Harry asked.

'What? No.' He puffed on the cigarette again. 'We liked to have a good time with women. They're hardly likely to go out with us if we look like we've fallen down a flight of concrete steps.'

'Any threats from anybody?'

'No. I didn't get any and I'm sure Clarkie would have told me if he had.'

'What about the people you work with?' Alex said. 'Did you fool around with any of the women here?'

'No. Don't get me wrong, there are a lot of available women, but you know what it's like when you go out with somebody at work and it goes belly up.'

'No, I don't know what that's like,' Harry said, maybe a little too quickly, sharing a look with Alex.

'Did you ever go out with married women?' Alex asked.

More sucking on the cigarette. Harry watched as a United plane took off from Edinburgh airport opposite, heading for New York.

'Yes. Only the ones who were up for it. We didn't want to break anybody up, but some of those married women go out on the town with one thing in mind. We're just supplying a service.'

'A service?' Alex said.

'Without guys like me, those women wouldn't be able to fool around on their spouses.'

'Are you married, Tommy?' Harry asked.

'Was. I cheated on her and we called it a day. That's when I started going out drinking with Clarkie after I found out what an animal he was.' He took one last drag on the cigarette and flicked it away. 'You should ask that daft bitch Sasha Young where she was on Friday. She was the closest thing he had to a regular girlfriend. Until he dumped her.'

'I was told she's off sick,' Harry said.

'I wouldn't know. I haven't seen her in a little while. But if you ask me, Clarkie did the right thing by dumping her. She was all giggles in the canteen until he started actually going out with her, then she became possessive. Wanted him to leave his wife.'

'What about Joe Leslie? You know him?' Harry had a quick look at his notebook to make sure he'd got the name right; Clark Naismith's ex-wife's new husband.

'I've seen him going about. He's pretty straight-laced though. Never goes out with the boys. He lives in Fife so he drives over and says he won't drink and drive.'

'You never saw him and Clark get into it?'

'What, Joe? Nah. He's a mild-mannered man. All-round good guy.'

'Thanks, Mr Gallagher. If you think of anything else, give us a call.' He handed Gallagher a business card before they got back into their car.

'Mild-mannered good guy,' Harry said. 'Until they get a knife in their hands. But I don't think that's a road we need to go down. Not yet.'

'Clark Naismith was an animal alright, and it might have been the death of him,' Alex said as they drove away.

FIFTEEN

'A'right, Arthur?' Ronnie Vallance said as he was shown into Arthur Daniels' office. 'How's the toy business doing these days?'

DC Gregg Simon stood beside him, actually managing to make Vallance look small.

'Mr Vallance! Good to see you again. Please, have a seat. Both of you.'

The detectives sat down opposite the smaller man, who had dark hair, thinning on top but nothing a little bit of strategic combing couldn't hide. He obviously came from a long line of Mediterranean ancestry.

'This is not a toy shop, as Mr Vallance puts it, but a collectors' emporium.' He beamed a smile. The toy shop was on Lothian Road round from the Usher Hall. 'Just like it says on the sign outside; *The Model Emporium*.'

'I always get that confused with the hoor house you've got next door,' Vallance said, smiling.

Daniels beamed a smile at them. 'Listen to him! Hoor house. What are you like? No, as I told you a long time ago, I got out of that game. Sold up. Moved on. I'm as happy as Larry playing with my toys all day.'

Vallance laughed and pointed a finger at him. He ran a hand through his beard. 'And yet I hear things, Arthur. Things that indicate that maybe you're going back to your old ways.'

Daniels managed to look offended. 'How can you say that about me?'

'I sit here, listening to you, giving you the benefit of the doubt, but once again, I have the same feeling I get when I catch my sixteen-year-old sons trying to sneak into the house at four in the morning.'

'What feeling is that?'

'That all is not right. That he's trying to pull the wool and them only sixteen an' all. Bloody wee rascals. Them, not you. But I tell them, I've been in the polis for twenty-five years. I'm not wet behind the ears.'

'Congratulations,' Daniels said, the smile coming back. 'Happy anniversary.'

Vallance couldn't tell if Daniels was taking the piss or not. 'Wait. I haven't finished.' He leaned forward and his ample gut touched the desk in front of him. 'I'm teaching the boy here and he's learning very quickly. Isn't that right, Simon?'

'It is indeed.'

Vallance leaned back in the chair, which protested alarmingly. 'And what have you learned this morning?' he asked Gregg.

'That Mr Daniels here is being rather frugal with the truth.'

'What?' Daniels almost threw himself back into his chair. 'I have to protest, Mr Vallance. You know I'm an honest businessman. I've moved on from my younger days. I keep my business clean and—'

'Platinum Escort Services,' Vallance said.

Daniels' smile faltered. 'What?'

'That hoor service you own.'

'Dearie me. What kind of talk is that in front of the young lad there? He might get the impression I'm a snake, if you keep talking like that.'

'You do have some resemblance to a reptile, Arthur, I have to admit.'

Daniels tutted and shook his head. 'My mother would roll in her grave right now if she—'

'Was dead. I saw her last week in Tesco. Looking very well for a woman in her seventies with a son who's a whoremaster.'

'Let me finish. I was going to say... if she was dead. That was a figure of speech.'

'Let's talk about Platinum, Arthur.' Vallance smiled, enjoying the dance.

'Just a little hobby, Mr Vallance. Like a retired gynaecologist, I like to keep my hand in.'

'Keep the jokes up, Arthur. Maybe you could tell one to the judge.'

'I jest, but Platinum isn't like the chain of saunas I had. Honestly. I saw an untapped niche and I jumped on it.'

'Untapped niche?'

'In my previous life, before I found religion, I saw men from all walks of life. All looking for one thing. But let me tell you a story. There was a vicar...'

Vallance laughed. 'What is this now? A vicar, a priest and a rabbi all walk into a bar?'

'No, really. Listen. Let me tell you this true story, and it doesn't involve a bar. This vicar I knew, he and I got talking at a party one night. It was one of those business dos that the wife gets invited to from time to time. Through her work.' He looked at Gregg. 'She's a consultant for a stationery company.'

'You digress,' Vallance said.

'Right. So we were at a dinner in this private room in a fancy hotel down in London, and this vicar says to me, I hear you have women working for you. I looked at him for a moment, thinking I was going to get a lecture, but he smiled at me and told me that's not what he wanted. No, he asked me if I knew anybody who had women he could hire for a couple of hours. He was coming up to give a talk, and had been invited along to a dinner afterwards, and somebody said he should bring his wife as all the wives were coming. His wife had died, and he felt like he was going to be like a spare pri... guest at a wedding.

'I told him I knew a woman who could be like his girlfriend for the night. *Evening* he told me with a smile. He just wanted the others to know he had somebody in his life, not necessarily a wife, but at least a girlfriend. He rehearsed a few things with her beforehand, and she pretended to be his other half. Nobody knew him there so they didn't know the difference.'

'Was this woman a regular sauna girl?' Gregg asked.

'She was, although I warned her, well, not to offer extended services to the old boy. This was one of my more mature girls, so she fit right in. She went along to the dinner and he dropped her into a cab later on. He paid me for my services and was delighted with the company. Told me I should offer this kind of service as some older blokes just wanted to rent some good-looking woman for an evening so they wouldn't look like some saddo at a do all by themselves. Hence, Platinum was born.'

'And all you offer is a true escort service?' Vallance said, his voice filled with scepticism.

'As God is my witness. And listen, this is a lucrative game. Those old blokes have plenty of dosh, and they don't mind splashing it around, let me tell you. Ask your vice department, they'll tell you they have no problems from me and my ladies. There's nothing underhand going on.'

'I already did, Arthur. Again, I'm not wet behind the ears.'

'Didn't mean to suggest you were. You two want a coffee? I'll have my assistant run out for some.'

'We're good,' Vallance said, answering for them both. He didn't want to risk the assistant gobbing in them. 'What can you tell me about Michelle Naismith?'

'Let me tell you, I was shocked to hear about her husband. Stabbed to death on his doorstep? Bloody hell. Makes me glad I've got Chloe to look after me.'

'Chloe?' Gregg asked.

'My Rottie. She's big and nasty.'

'Like your wife,' Vallance added.

'Aw, come on, Mr Vallance. That was one time. And it was that certain time when a lady becomes a laddie, all feisty and moody, like when they're juiced up on jelly shots and go up the town looking for a fight.'

'She said she'd sink her teeth into my arse, because there was enough of it.'

Gregg let out a snigger.

'That's not funny, son. I'd rather take my chances with his dog. But again, you're going off at a tangent.'

'Right. Naismith... stabbed. Jesus. Poor Michelle. I can't even imagine. She dropped me in it on Saturday night, though. I had to get Naomi to step in, and she was starting to come down with a cold. It was like having my client go out with typhoid Mary. Just as well he was taking her to a wedding reception in the evening, and not wanting to do the nasty. I would have told him to find business elsewhere if that had been the case. Still, he was pissed off and I had to give him a fifty per cent reduction and a coupon for the next time.'

'You give coupons?' Gregg asked.

'Aye. You interested?'

'No. I'm just surprised, that's all. My mother cuts out coupons, but never for Hoors 'R' Us.'

'Hey, what way is that to talk about my ladies? They're all respectable women. Including Michelle Naismith. I can't tell you much about her, I'm afraid.'

'Aye, Gregg, what's that all about?' Vallance said. 'This man runs a legitimate business. As I'm sure the HM Revenue and Customs will confirm.'

'Whoa, whoa, let's not get hysterical here,' Daniels said. He sat back in his chair. 'Yes, Michelle Naismith. What can I say about her? She's good-looking, smart, takes care of herself and knows how to have a conversation other than *Do want to add some extras?* She's a real asset to my company.'

'Did she have any problems with your customers?' Gregg asked.

'I prefer to call them clients, but tomatoes, tomaytoes.' He spread his hands in a gesture of *who's counting?* 'But no, not that I was aware of. I won't stand for that sort of nonsense, but my clients are generally older fellas who need to have a piece of eye candy on their arm for a social occasion, as we already discussed.'

'Did she say what her husband thought about her doing that sort of thing?' Vallance said.

'Again with the inference that this is some sort of mucky business, Mr Vallance. Her husband was quite happy to have her out of the house, I gather. She knew he would go out and entertain other women. Dirty bastard. I've been married for over thirty years and never once looked at another woman. And I've been surrounded by them. But each to his own, I suppose.'

'Did she say if they were having any money issues?' Gregg said.

'Not to me. I pay my girls well. I also charge the clients a fair bob or two, but you get what you pay for. If you want some company that throws in a free trip to the doctor after your pee starts to burn, then by all means, take out Smelly Susie. But if all you want is a nice night out with a beautiful woman on your arm, then I'm your man. I fix them up, Mr Vallance, and no mistake. And the women are all taken care of.'

Vallance sat looking at the other man for a moment to see if he was hiding something, but Daniels looked like he was telling the truth.

'Okay, Arthur, we won't take up any more of your time, but if something does come to mind after we're gone...'

'I'll be sure to call you directly, Mr Vallance.'

The detectives stood up, Gregg leading the way out of the office.

'Just before you go, Mr Vallance,' Arthur said.

The two men stopped but Vallance nodded for Gregg to go ahead without him.

'You mentioned HM Revenue earlier. I mean, well... you know...'

'Relax, Arthur. I'm a busy man to be running to those bastards. I'd only do that if I thought you were taking the piss.'

'Thank you. Not that I've anything to worry about, you understand, but those people have a bigger bite than my Chloe.'

'Just stay out of trouble. Keep on playing with your toys.' He turned and walked out of the office. He caught up to Gregg who was standing in the street looking in one of the big windows.

'I used to make Airfix planes. Me and my mates,' Vallance said. 'Nowadays, it's all computer games with kids. Sitting in front of a TV instead of being out with their pals. No wonder they get rickets.'

'I didn't know there was an epidemic, sir.'

'Give it time, son, give it time.'

SIXTEEN

'I was thinking of wearing a kilt to our wedding,' Harry said as they pulled into the car park at the Fettes station.

'Whoa, back it up a bit there; we aren't even engaged.'

He smiled at her. 'We've talked about getting married though, haven't we?'

'It has been mentioned in passing conversation.'

'You browse wedding sites online. You've started a wedding list.'

'You haven't asked me yet, Harry.'

'Okay, but I'm just jumping ahead here. I know I want you to be my wife.'

'You're a big sap.' She squeezed his hand. 'But I love you too. There is one thing you haven't considered when thinking about a kilt.'

'What's that?'

'You have to be over eighteen to look at those legs. You might be able to get a special licence or something, but my old Auntie Ina will faint if she sees them. Young kids would run away screaming.'

'I'm not shaving them, if that's what you're hinting at. These are burly Scotsman's legs, and tae the Lord we thank it.'

'You could always make prints of your legs so people could hang them above the fire to keep the bairns away.'

'Talking about hair, maybe we should talk about who has the better moustache.'

'What? Don't be a pig, McNeil.' They went inside the building. 'I don't have a noticeable moustache, do I?'

'You put Billy Connolly to shame.'

'Wait; he has a beard as well.'

Harry raised his eyebrows. 'Just saying.'

'Oh, go away with yourself.'

He laughed as they took the lift up to the MIT level.

Inside the incident room, Ronnie Gallagher was with the rest of the team.

'How'd you get on?' he asked Vallance.

'Michelle Naismith was working as an escort, but not one of the usual kind, where money was handed over for special services at the end of the night. According to Arthur Daniels.'

'Arthur Daniels? That's what he specialised in, back in the day.'

'He says the non-sex worker type is more lucrative. Seems he created a niche for himself. Tapped into a service that people wanted but nobody was supplying.'

'What did he say about Michelle's personal life?' Karen Shiels asked. 'Anything?'

'No, nothing to write home about. Says she didn't talk about domestics or anything.'

'Somebody had it in for Clark, that's for sure.'

'His friend, Tommy Gallagher said there was no fighting or any problems in the bar they were in on Friday,' Harry said. 'Did you talk with the manager?'

'Yes,' Eve said. 'There were no fights.'

'If this was a hit, then there had to be a reason behind it. Let's get this stuff up on the whiteboard. Get some kind of timeline going.'

They bustled about, posting notes and photos up on the board. Then Harry stood in front of them. 'This is what we've got so far; Clark Naismith came home from the pub, having been out with some colleagues from work. There were no reported fights or arguments. His family were at home, where his wife, Michelle, was waiting to go out with her sister. There was a commotion at the door then young Dennis, the son, heard a scream from his mother as she opened the door and found her husband had been stabbed. Her sister, Linda, came running up and tried to help him. The attacker was running away from the house. We know from both Michelle and Dennis that a man has been watching the house. The son got a photo but the stranger was wearing a baseball cap and had his collar pulled up. Facial recognition hasn't come up with anything. We got uniforms to ask door-to-door about him. What's the result on that, Eve?'

'Nothing, I'm afraid. Nobody reported seeing anybody lurking about opposite the Naismiths'. Which is not surprising because the park is used by dog walkers, so if anybody is seen in there, more often than not, they have a dog. It doesn't stick out.'

'Anything else on the red Astra?'

'We're still looking, still searching for CCTVs in the area,' Karen Shiels said.

'Keep on that. And for Ronnie's benefit, we had a witness say a man was running along Naismith's street, and he jumped into a red Astra driven by somebody else, so we're working that angle. If it was our man, he has an accomplice.'

'What about forensics?' Vallance asked.

'They've taken blood samples from the scene,' Gregg answered. 'They're checking them against Clark and Michelle so they can identify any stray spatters from the killer, in case he cut himself.'

'Prints?'

'Still being analysed.'

Harry sat on the corner of a desk. 'We can only hope he got careless and touched something, but if this was a pro, we won't find anything.'

'If it was a pro, I'd like to know *why* somebody sent a hitman to take care of Naismith,' Vallance said.

'We spoke to his colleagues today, and we'll talk to another one who is off sick, but it seems Clark and his wingman Tommy Gallagher liked to put it about. We also interviewed their respective exes and their alibis pan out, so they're not suspects.'

'We're not ruling out that it might be the husband of one of the women Clark was messing about with.'

'I also want some of the immediate family members interviewed. Like Clark's mum and dad. Can you get on that, Ronnie? Take Eve with you. Let her get out and get some fresh air. Alex and I will talk to Michelle again. Karen, can you and Simon see if you can find that Astra?'

He stood up off the desk and stretched.

'Maybe we should get an opinion from Michelle's parents,' Ronnie said.

'They're deceased. Both of them. A car accident a few months ago. But I want to go and talk to the sister, Linda, in her own place.' He turned to Eve. 'I assume we have details for her in the system?'

'We do. Here, I'll print it out,' she said, her fingers moving deftly over the keyboard.' A few seconds later, the printer spat the paper out with Linda Hogan's name and address on it. Harry folded it and put it in his pocket.

They all split into their teams and made their way out.

'I was just thinking about what you said earlier,' Harry said.

'About what?' Alex said as they made their way across to the little red Audi.

'About what, she says. Don't act all coy and innocent with me.'

'About your legs looking like a shag rug?'

'Yes. Screw the kilt. I'll wear a tux.'

'Aw, come on, I was only pulling your leg. If you see what I mean.'

They got in the car. 'No, I mean it. It was a stupid idea anyway. When I got married the first time, I wore a kilt.'

Alex started the car and pulled out of the parking space. 'Well, maybe you should wear a tux for our wedding then. It would be unique, for us. And all those women who would have vomited—'

'Swooned.'

'...over your legs will just have to go without a peek. I still think you should go with the photo thing for keeping the bairns away from the fire. Just saying.'

'Just drive, sergeant. We'll talk about this when we get home. And don't think you'll be getting to rifle through my Jimmy Shand collection anytime soon.'

'Is that a euphemism for something?'

'No it's bloody well not. You think you're going to put one of my grandfather's LPs on and dance about when your blootered, just think again.'

'I've never shown an interest in doing that,' she said, grinning.

'Just as well as I don't have a record player anymore.'

'Listen to Uncle Harry, forty going on sixty. Record player. Kids nowadays would laugh at you. Next time you go to a school to give one of those school crossing patrol talks, try not to talk about record players.'

'You'll be on school crossing patrol, missy, if I get any more of your lip.'

'Just remember who has the real power in this relationship, Chief Inspector.' She grinned at him again.

'Damnit,' he said, looking out the window. 'Fine. Go ahead. Rifle through my collection.'

'See? That was easy.'

SEVENTEEN

'I was sorry to hear what happened to your wife and daughter, pal,' Ronnie Vallance said to Simon Gregg as they got in the car.

'Aye. Thanks. It was sudden. That was a mercy, anyway. They were both killed outright. The other driver was drunk. Ironically, he walked away without a scratch.'

'You'll be glad to know that bastard who ordered you to the cold case unit is gone now. Last I heard, he was in the Met, and a buddy of mine down there said they treat him like shite. They're trying to force the bastard to quit.'

'He's no job being in uniform.'

'Aye, well, hopefully not for much longer. I'm glad you stuck it out though, Simon. I've heard good things about you.'

Gregg jammed the brakes on at the exit to the car park.

'Maybe not about your driving, right enough.'

Gregg grinned as he pulled out and headed along Ferry Road and down to Trinity.

'What about you, sir? You enjoying being with MIT?'

'Aye. Harry McNeil put in a word for me. He and I go way back. Some of those other backstabbing bastards would throw him off a cliff for being in Professional Standards, but not me. If you keep your nose clean, then there's no need to fear Standards giving it to you sideways, is there?'

'I suppose not.'

'Trust me, son, keep your nose clean and you'll go far. You're already a valued member of MIT, and if Harry didn't want you on his team, you wouldn't be here.'

Gregg drove along South Trinity Road until it became Sterling Road. The house they were looking for was on the left. A quick phone call told them the occupants would be at home when they visited.

The house was an end-terrace villa with a double garage tacked onto the side. Gregg pulled into the small drive in front of the garage doors and stopped.

'At least you didn't put the car through it,' Vallance said, getting out of the car and Gregg felt the weight shift.

Inside, Clark Naismith's parents were waiting for them. If Vallance didn't know better, he might have thought that Naismith's mother was a junkie, her eyes were so red. She looked like she hadn't stopped crying since she heard the news about her son's death.

'Have you found his killer?' she asked, a cotton hanky in one hand, ready to spring into action.

'I'm afraid not,' Vallance said. 'This is just a follow-up interview. We're doing everything we can to catch your son's killer, but it takes time. That's why we want to ask you some more questions.'

Vallance and Gregg sat on a settee and the parents sat in chairs, looking at the detectives like they were double glazing salesmen come to rob them of their savings.

'I know this is very upsetting,' Vallance started, 'but we need to go over everything. With that in mind, can you think of any time that Clark got into trouble recently?'

'What sort of trouble?' Clarke's father asked.

'Like, say, a fight at the pub, or at work? Or involved in road rage?'

'Oh, no, Clark would never get into any trouble. He didn't get into fights.'

'Not that he would tell you,' the mother said, looking at her husband.

'What are you trying to say? That Clark got into brawls?'

'Not brawls in the pub, but he did get into an argument that one time.'

'What time was this, Mrs Naismith?' Gregg said.

The mother looked at him. 'That time he got into an argument with that thug from Glasgow.' She sniffed and dabbed at her eyes again.

Vallance had seen this before, where a relative started to get overwhelmed with grief and shut down. He wanted to make sure the old woman didn't. 'What thug was that?'

'The one that Michelle was married to.' She looked him in the eye. 'Why couldn't he leave them alone? They were happy together. Yet her ex-husband wouldn't leave them alone.'

'Did Clark get into a fight with him? Trevor Avery? Did he tell you about it?'

'No. It was Michelle who told me about him.'

'When was this?' Gregg asked.

'Not long ago. She said she didn't want Clark to find out but she didn't want to keep it bottled up so she confided in us. Maybe he murdered my son.'

'He has an alibi for the evening in question. But do you know what the problem was?'

'That son of hers. Right little hooligan he is. We could never think of him as our grandchild. He's...' She looked at her husband for help.

'A rascal,' the father offered. Vallance was about to suggest *little bastard* but kept it to himself.

'In what way?' he asked instead.

'He was always acting up. His mother gave him everything and then when Clark came along, he acted even more spoiled. She couldn't control him. His father took him some weekends, which gave them peace, especially after the baby came along.'

'Was he jealous of the little girl?' Gregg asked.

'Yes. And when he saw them giving her things, it made him worse. You wouldn't believe she could have given birth to two such different children.'

'She didn't,' Vallance said.

'What do you mean?' she said, an edge of anger and shock ready to replace the tears.

'I mean, Trevor Avery had a one-year-old son when he met Michelle. She was his step-mum but she adopted him. That's why she got custody after the divorce. She's not his biological mother. She died when he was an infant.'

Mother clasped a hand to her chest as if she was struggling for breath. 'No wonder he was acting up. That explains a lot. Not even her flesh and blood. Well, she can keep him. I don't want anything else to do with him.'

'Did he get along with your son?'

'Yes, he seemed to get along. He was just acting like a typical teenager. It's different when it's your own flesh and blood though. To have somebody else's offspring act up like that while they're away enjoying the good life, well, it's difficult.'

'Did he ever act violent, that you know of?' Gregg asked.

'Not that I was ever told, but you don't know what goes on behind closed doors, do you?'

'When was the last time you saw Clark?' Vallance asked.

'Last week. Wednesday.' The woman's lip trembled. 'I want to see him. One last time.'

'That can be arranged. I'll have an officer from CID take you down to the mortuary. We can arrange a time.'

'Did Clark have any siblings?' Gregg asked.

'No. He was an only child. And now I don't have any.' She started crying again.

'Did Clark ever discuss his work with you?' Vallance asked.

'No. He worked in the bank. It wasn't exactly trying to find a cure for cancer,' the father said. 'He was lucky to get that job. If it wasn't for Michelle, he'd be stacking shelves in Sainsbury's. He was damn lucky to have her.'

'Did you know if he had a girlfriend on the side?' He threw it out there, like throwing a hand grenade, and hoped it wasn't going to blow up in his face. He expected mother to bluster and father to start protesting loudly while adding a pointing finger for good measure, suggesting the detectives leave the house.

But none of that came.

They looked at each other before looking at Vallance. 'Yes. We knew about her, and we tried to get him to stop seeing her,' the old man answered.

'Do you know who it was?' Gregg asked.

'Yes. Her name was Briony Dixon.'

EIGHTEEN

Michelle Naismith's sister lived in Oxgangs, in a block of flats that had seen better days. Some of the harling had fallen off, exposing the brick underneath.

Alex parked her car and they went into the block. It was dank, and smelled. A man opened his door and was about to step out when he saw Harry and hurriedly stepped back inside and shut the door.

'It's the polis,' they heard him say to whoever else was in there with him.

A female. She raised her voice. 'What you been up to now?'

'Nothin',' he answered.

Harry got the feeling a domestic was about to get underway, with the man being on the receiving end.

They found Linda Hogarth's door and Harry knocked on it. It opened a few moments later, a woman's face peering round the gap, the security chain the only thing between her and safety.

'What?'

'Linda? I'm DCI Harry McNeil. This is DS Alex...'

The door closed and the chain was slid off and the door opened again. Harry felt he could have just blown the small chain off, for all the good it was doing. Maybe it held a lot of psychological value.

'I remember who you are.'

Linda lit up a cigarette in the living room, making a half-hearted attempt at tidying up by piling some newspapers into a heap then firing them down onto a dining chair. There was no sign of a dining table and Harry wondered if the chair was kept there for the purpose of holding the newspapers when visitors came round.

'Sit,' Linda barked, then proceeded to attempt to donate a lung by coughing it up.

Alex was wondering if they had actually got the right address.

'We wanted to talk to you about Clark's murder,' Harry said, trying not to turn his nose up.

'What about it? You know where I was Friday evening; on my hands and knees trying to stop the blood from pouring out of his chest.'

'Before that.' He scanned the room, looking for any place that would have acted as a seating area should he change his mind, but there was nothing obvious.

'I got an Uber and he stopped two doors down, the prick. I told him what house to stop at but he was in such a bloody hurry to get away again, I just got out. It was only a short walk to my sisters.' She glared at them as if daring them to contradict her.

'Were you coming from home, or work?'

'I don't go out for a drink with my sister wearing my uniform, for God's sake. I did manage to get a shower before I met her.'

'And where do you work?' Alex asked.

'In a nursing home.'

'We'll need details.'

Linda tutted and reached for a small pad and pen that sat on a cluttered side table at the end of the settee. She wrote something down, and much to Harry's surprise, it was legible.

'Did you hear anything about anybody wanting to harm Clark?' Alex asked.

'No. Why should I?'

'Maybe because his wife is your sister.'

Linda shrugged and put her lips round the cigarette like she was making a duck face. Duck's arse, more like, Harry thought. He hadn't met anybody so obnoxious in a long time.

'Sister's talk about that sort of thing,' he said to Linda.

'You have a sister, do you?'

'No, I have a brother, and we share things.' He

didn't want to admit he had a sister. It was none of Linda's business.

'Good for you. Michelle and I are not close. Not since... the incident.'

Harry and Alex shared a look before Harry pressed on. 'What incident?'

More smoking, more blowing smoke into the room.

'There's more than one.' She looked at Harry, as if expecting him to have a guess.

'Go on,' he said.

'We used to be close, until she lost the baby.'

'Was this with her first husband, Trevor?' Alex asked.

Linda shook her head. 'No. It was with Clark. She was gutted. I was surprised she even wanted another baby.'

'What other incident?' Harry said, not wanting the woman to clam up now.

The cigarette bobbed up and down as she spoke around it. 'Our parents died.'

'I read that. A car accident, wasn't it?'

Linda's eyebrows did their best to meet in the middle and called it quits halfway. She took the cigarette out of her mouth. 'Is that what Michelle told you?'

'Yes.'

'Well, there *was* a car involved. But car accident? It certainly wasn't an accident.'

'What do you mean?' Alex asked.

Linda made a face like she was disgusted that Alex didn't know about this. 'They killed themselves. Went into the garage, turned on their car with a hosepipe attached to the exhaust, and sat waiting to be taken to another place. They were both very much dead by the time a neighbour called the police to say she was worried about them.'

'When did this happen?' Harry asked.

'About three months ago. Give or take.'

'That's tragic,' Alex said.

'You think? It's bad enough that one of your parents dies, but both of them on the same day by suicide? I don't know how Michelle was able to carry on after that. I've been a wreck.'

'You got kids?' Harry asked.

'Nope.' More duck-face cigarette smoking.

'That's how she managed to carry on. When you have kids, you dig deep.'

'That wasn't the case for our parents. They had two girls. Why would you want to leave your two daughters?'

Harry didn't have the answer.

'I'm surprised Michelle wanted to have a kid with Clark in the first place. She told me she had adopted Dennis and that was enough for her. She never wanted to get pregnant the first time, never mind a second time, not after losing the baby. She couldn't go through that again. But she ended up with Chloe, and she's been fine. Michelle worried about nothing. God, every second of every day, she was worried about that baby before she was even born. She was convinced she was going to die, like the first one.'

'Did your parents have any problems? Financial or otherwise?' Alex asked.

'No. They were happy. They lived on their property in a quiet village. They were retired with years of life left in them.'

'Something triggered it. People just don't wake up one morning and decide to take their own lives. There's usually some sort of build up.'

'I don't have the answer,' Linda said. 'I wish I did.'

'What were their names?'

She told them.

'Again, we're sorry for your loss,' Harry said, indicating to Alex that they were going to leave.

'There is one thing,' Linda said as Harry started to move.

'What's that?'

'It might be nothing. Probably is nothing.'

'Tell me anyway.'

'A developer wanted their house and the land to build on. They sold it to them. They were going to buy a house in Spain but weren't sure how Brexit would affect them. Something to do with the tax laws changing. They were looking at their options. One of those options was apparently killing themselves.'

'You and your sister were beneficiaries?'

'We didn't kill them for their money, if that's what you're thinking,' Linda said, her scowl returning.

'It happens more often than you think.'

'Michelle and I have alibis for that day. We loved our parents.' For the first time, Linda showed emotion and tears rolled down her cheeks.

'If you think of anything else, please give us a call,' Harry said, giving her a business card.

Outside, Harry's phone rang. It was Karen Shiels.

'Believe it or not, we got a hit on the perv who was watching the Naismiths' house the night Clark was murdered. A red Astra pulled into a petrol station, and the camera inside the shop in the station got a clear look at his face. One of our computer boys enhanced it enough to get a hit from facial recognition.'

'Good work. You got an address?'

She read it out to him, then he told Alex when they got in the car.

'What do you think of Linda?' Alex asked.

'I never would have pegged her for being Michelle's sister. And working in an old folk's home?' Harry thought it had to be on the cleaning crew. Surely somebody with Linda's sunshine personality would be overpowering for the old folks.

NINETEEN

The sun was out but clouds floated overhead, casting shadows for a brief moment before moving on.

There were no funerals going on in the cemetery so the man was easy to find. His wife had said he would be here.

Alex stopped the car close by, giving them enough room to prepare should the figure decide to rush them, but the man in question merely stood with his head bowed, one hand on top of the gravestone. He didn't look up until he realised Harry was standing close to him.

His eyes were red and tears were streaming down his face.

'Mr Michaels?' Harry asked.

Peter Michaels nodded. 'I was expecting you. Not here, but at my house. I knew it was only a matter of time.' He took his hand off the grave and looked down at the name. 'We called her Angelina because she was an angel sent from God. I was forty and my wife thirty-eight. We thought we'd never have kids, and when she got pregnant, I was over the moon.'

'Mr Michaels, we need you to come with us to our station at Fettes. Did you come here in a car?' Alex said.

'No, I walked. I'm assuming you know I live just around the corner?'

'Your wife said you'd be here.'

They got into Alex's car and drove out of Corstorphine Hill cemetery and headed back to their office.

Peter Michaels sat with a cup of water, cradling it with both hands, looking down at the table.

Harry got the recordings going, while Alex sat next to him.

'You're not under arrest, Mr Michaels. You can leave anytime. Do you understand that?'

Michaels looked at him. 'Yes.'

'Right, then, let's start at the beginning; why were you standing outside the Naismiths' home?'

Silence for a moment, and Harry thought the man wasn't going to speak, but then he took a sip of water and looked at the detectives.

'As I said to you in the cemetery, Angelina being born was a miracle. We'd tried for a baby for a long time, but nothing came of it. Of course, my wife suggested we try and get IV treatment, but I said no. That isn't the way God intended us to have children. If we couldn't have one, then that was God's way. She was upset, but agreed with my decision.

'Then she fell pregnant. She was over the moon, saying I was right all along. Everything was going well. It was a normal pregnancy. Smooth sailing. Then Angelina came into the world and she was beautiful. A gift from God. But then something didn't seem quite right. Suddenly, she didn't want to breast feed. The nurse said that sometimes happened. I thought it strange. I didn't think that was normal, but I'm no doctor, and they're the experts. She went onto bottle feeding.' He drank some more of the water and looked at Harry.

'Take your time, Mr Michaels.'

Michaels nodded before carrying on. 'We didn't think any more about it. That's when something happened. I can't remember all the exact details, but she had to see a specialist. This was when she was about two weeks old. They did a scan on her and it turned out she had a defective heart. She would need surgery, but they wanted to wait until she was a little bit older, another couple of months. They said she would be okay until then, but she would be closely monitored. Turns out her heart wasn't as strong as they'd thought, and it stopped. They couldn't do anything to bring her back, so we had to say goodbye to her. She lived for one month and one day.'

Alex felt a catch in her throat but cleared it before speaking. 'Where do the Naismiths fit into all of this?'

Michaels played with the cup. 'I said that the baby looked different at the time she stopped taking breast milk. I was right; Angelina wasn't our baby. She had been swapped.'

'How can that be?' Alex said. 'There's so much security nowadays.'

'I have no idea how it was done.'

'When did you find out? And *how* did you find out?' Harry asked.

'I got a phone call. I don't know how she found my number, but her name was Briony. Briony Dixon.'

TWENTY

'This is my house! Now get out!' Margaret shouted.

'But we all know that's not correct, don't we, Margaret?' Briony Dixon puffed on her cigarette and blew the smoke into the room.

'What's going on here?' Derek O'Neil said, coming into the living room.

'Your mum and I were talking about living arrangements, and I told her about us. She's not happy at all.'

'How could you?' Margaret said to Derek. 'She's practically your sister.'

She turned to look at Derek, who was standing in the middle of the room in nothing but boxers and a T-shirt. His hair was ruffled and he was unshaven.

'She's not my sister, for God's sake. She's your boyfriend's daughter.'

'I explained to your mum that you and I want to

live here, and suggested she go back to her own house in Rosyth, but she's having none of it.'

'You can't just kick my mother out. She owns the house.'

Briony smiled at him. 'If only that were true, eh, Margaret? I heard you tell your other son that you put up half the cost of this place. But that wasn't quite true, was it?'

Derek looked puzzled. 'You said you did. And whoever died first, the house would go to the other one. That's what you told me.'

'Do you want to tell him, or shall I?'

Margaret looked at the carpet for a moment before looking at her son. 'She's right. I thought Bobby owned this place You see, I told you and Harry that I owned this house, but the truth is, I don't. I wanted to do up my other place and sell it, but it takes money. I explained this to Bobby, but he just wanted to make me happy. I thought he had bought this place but it turns out he didn't. Briony is the actual owner. There's nothing I can do, son. She owns the house, not me.'

Derek looked at her. 'Is this true?'

Briony smirked and sucked on her cigarette. 'It is. My dad couldn't afford a house like this. He wasn't a fantastic businessman. Oh, he got by, but more by luck than anything else. No, me and my first husband bought this place and he died of cancer, and the mort-gage was paid off. He just wanted you to think he owned this place. He and Margaret moved in with me, not the other way round. I'm sure they told you they had bought this place, but they hadn't. Although I love you, Derek, I'm afraid my father didn't trust you. He just put up with you. I mean, he sort of had a point. You moved in here after he disappeared, because he wouldn't have allowed it if he was still alive.'

'I thought he liked me?' Derek managed to look like a hurt little boy.

'Oh, lover, he did like you. He just didn't trust you. There's a big difference.'

Derek looked at her. 'What about you? Do you trust me?'

'Of course. When your mother leaves here, we'll have this big place to ourselves.'

'This is sick,' Margaret said. 'How can you even think about staying here with your brother?'

'He's not my brother. Besides, it's not like we're children. We're adults. Derek and I love each other. Don't we, honey?'

Derek looked like a deer caught in the headlights. 'Yeah.' He looked at his mother. 'Yes, we do, and if you're not happy, then we don't care.' The words rushed out of him like some kind of drug had just kicked in.

Briony laughed. 'Oh, we don't want you to leave right away. We won't see you out on the street, but you have to understand, we want to start our own lives. You've been here for three months since my dad disappeared, and I did warn you way back when.'

Derek looked at her. 'I hope you understand this isn't personal...'

'Save it, Derek. You just want a roof over your head. You were quite happy to stay here with me, but now you realise that she owns the house, you're going to stay with her.'

'You're wrong! We've been a couple for a while now,' he said.

'Since when? Since Bobby went missing?'

'Before that. We just kept it a secret.'

'Did he find out?' Margaret asked.

Derek looked between the two women, waiting for Briony to answer.

'Not from me,' Briony answered.

'Don't look at me. That's hardly the sort of conversation I could have had with him. *Oh, and by the way, I'm banging your daughter.* Pass me the cornflakes box.'

'Don't be crude, Derek,' Briony said.

'Sorry.' He looked at his mother. 'Look, it just happened. Briony's right; we're not kids, we're not related. At the end of the day, you weren't married, were you?'

'We hadn't signed the papers, no, but that doesn't mean we weren't husband and wife. We considered ourselves to be married.'

'Just not in the eyes of the law.' Derek gave her his best pathetic look.

'How did you find out?'

'I just...'

'That's not important,' Briony said. 'Derek and I are going to be together, and I hope we have your blessing.'

'You'll never have that.' Margaret stood looking at them both before walking out of the living room.

'I need to go and talk to my brother. You'll be okay staying here, I hope?' Derek said.

'Of course.'

'I'm going to ask to crash at Harry's flat. I'm sure he'll be amenable to it.' He looked at her. 'You haven't got any cash have you?'

TWENTY-ONE

'No, you can't crash at my place,' Harry said, putting two pint glasses down on the table.

'Aw, come on. Now that Alex has moved into your room, there's a spare bed.' He picked up a pint and clinked it against his brother's.

'No. You're lucky I came out for a pint at all.' They were in the St Bernard's in Raeburn Place, one of Harry's regular haunts. There were the usual suspects in, men who weren't giving a second thought to their livers.

'I'm not going to beg you, Harry.'

'Glad to hear it.'

Derek paused for a few seconds. 'Okay, I'm begging you. Satisfied? You must feel proud, waiting to hear your own flesh and blood begging. What has it come down to when a grown man has to beg?'

'Oh, for God's sake. If it's the money, I'll pay an

Uber for you. But no extras for puking in the back. That's all on you.'

'It's not the money. I have money on me.'

'I wish you'd get to the point. This is our third pint and still you haven't spilled why you think Bobby Dixon was murdered. Or is this your overactive imagination at work again?'

'I've been hesitant to tell you because you're not going to believe me.'

Harry looked at him. He'd had reservations about meeting for a pint, but had decided to give his brother the benefit of the doubt. Now he wasn't so sure.

'Tell me and I'll reserve judgement until you're done.'

'Alright. Here we go, but hear me out mind; I think our mother killed Bobby.'

'What? Aw Jesus, I knew it. Bloody drivel.'

'You know what, Harry? If you could climb down from your own arse for a second and listen, maybe you would understand. You're supposed to be a bloody detective.'

'Okay, okay, I'll listen until the end.' Harry drank some of his pint and hoped his scepticism wasn't showing on his face.

'When I spoke to you on the phone, I told you strange things were happening in the house, not long after Bobby disappeared. Like things moving and the manky footprint in the kitchen.'

'I remember.'

'I also told you Bobby had been arguing with Clark Naismith at the front door. Well, I think Mum hired somebody to get rid of Bobby.'

Whatever Harry had been expecting to come out of Derek's mouth, it certainly wasn't this. 'You think our mother was responsible for the death of her husband?'

'Yes. And he wasn't her husband. Common-law husband, maybe, but not actual husband. They told the story of how they went away to the Highlands and got hitched, but that was all pish. They went away for a dirty weekend. That was it. When they needed a place to stay, they moved in with Briony, who owns the house. They told people they bought it. Including us, but that was all pish too.'

Harry took some of his lager and contemplated for a moment. 'How long have you known?'

'Since Briony wanted to go out with me. I thought she was crazy, but she sat down with me and explained. I went to Register House and couldn't find any marriage certificate. Today, when we were talking to Mum, she admitted it.'

'You and Briony?' Harry turned his face up at the news.

'Mum got mad at her but she really has no right to. It's Briony's house, bought by her and her dead husband.'

'What's Mum going to do?'

'Briony asked her to leave.'

'Christ, Derek, you're going to throw our mother out onto the street?'

'No, it's not like that. Mum is going to get her own place, that's all. It's not like we're going to see her in a cardboard box.'

'I'm sure Briony would love that.'

'Funerals are an emotional time, Harry.'

'Okay, but how does that make Mum a murderer?'

'She found out about the house and she realised that she would get nothing if he died. Maybe she was pissed off about that and killed him in a fight. I don't know. They don't pay me to figure out puzzles like they do you. However, you said that Bobby had a fractured skull. From falling and hitting rocks, most likely, and so foul play was ruled out, especially since they saw the state of the body. But she was the last one who saw him alive.'

'That we know of,' Harry said.

'Oh, come on. Nobody came forward to say they had seen him after it went on the news. Mum was the last one.'

Harry didn't look at his brother. He wanted to look at anybody else but his brother right then. How could Derek come out with such nonsense? But it was eating away at him. What if he was right? He'd seen some tragic things in his time as a copper, especially things that one spouse could do to another. It never surprised him what some human beings could do to others.

'What were they like with each other when you

moved in?' he asked, hating himself for doing so. To ask meant he was entertaining the idea that their mother was a killer.

'They were fine. At first. But things went downhill fast. I don't know what they were like when they first got together. They were with each other for over two years I think, and I assume they got on fine, or else they would have split up.'

'There had to have been a catalyst, Derek. Some spark had to light the fire.'

'The only thing I saw, that I already told you about, was that guy Clark coming round to the house. You should ask his wife what he was doing there.'

'I will. But how do I know Briony didn't kill Bobby and you're covering for her?'

'She has an alibi for the night he went missing – me. We went out to dinner that night and we went home together. I went home with her and stayed the night. I moved in shortly after that. That's how it all started with her and me. But we stayed up late, then I spent the night. But Mum went out to look for Bobby. I think she found him.'

Harry felt sick to his stomach, but he was going to reserve judgement before acting on it.

'Have you decided if I can stay tonight?' Derek asked. 'I think we could mend some bridges, brother. Mel would be happy about it too. The three siblings together again.'

'That flat isn't just mine anymore. Here, ask my

better half.' He took out his phone and dialled Alex's number and held the phone out.

After Derek asked her, he smiled and handed the phone back. 'You've got a good 'un there, Harry.'

'Crap. I thought she'd say no.'

'Too late to take it back now. Let me get another round in.'

'You're up when we're up and you're leaving when we leave. We're babysitting a cat and I don't want him upset.'

'Fine by me. I like cats.'

TWENTY-TWO

Margaret O'Neil stood looking out of her living room window at the Forth rail bridge in the distance. She thought about how her life had come down to this. The man she'd thought of as her husband was gone now, she wouldn't have a home shortly, and her son was quite happy to see her out on the street.

She would miss this place. It had been her home for a while now. Maybe her daughter would take her in. Maybe Harry, but it wasn't fair on him. He was just starting his life with Alex and the last thing they wanted was an old woman living with them. No, she would take it on the chin. She still had her first husband's pension. That would see her through. She'd get a place to rent, just a little flat so she could get a cat.

She took out her cigarettes and lit one. Bobby would be annoyed if he could see her now, polluting their living room with the foul smoke. She sat down on one of the big, overstuffed chairs and switched the TV on. Flipped through the channels, unable to concentrate on anything in particular.

She thought about her two boys, going out for a drink together. It made her proud of Harry. She knew he'd had to dig deep to be able to talk to Derek after the words they'd had years ago after their father died. It wasn't easy on any of them, especially their sister Mel, who had been a daddy's girl. But the drink had consumed him, and his daughter had watched as her older brother had seemed to encourage him, but deep down, Margaret knew it wasn't Harry's fault. He just wanted to have a drink with his father. Maybe that's why he became a copper in the end, to show his father he could be just like him, but the truth of the matter was, Harry was a much better man.

She sensed somebody behind her.

'Come to gloat, have you?' she asked, turning round.

She'd expected to see Briony, but it wasn't her.

'What are you doing here?' Margaret said, her heart beating faster.

'Aren't you going to offer me a drink?'

'I'm going to offer you nothing, but I am going to tell you to get the hell out of my house.'

'That's not very nice. And I think you should be nice to me, Margaret.'

'Why should I be nice to you? Just get out and I won't call the police.'

'I don't think you'll call the police. You don't want them digging through your life. You know what I'm doing here. It's time we had a talk.'

'About what?' They locked eyes, and Margaret saw the smile, totally devoid of humour, and filled with evil.

'About who really killed Bobby.'

TWENTY-THREE

'That wasn't so bad, was it?' Alex said as she put the kettle on for their morning coffee. 'Your brother's quite a good laugh when he has a drink in him.'

'It went better than expected,' he grudgingly admitted. 'If it hadn't been for the fact that he thinks my mother's a serial killer.'

'You said he'll be leaving when we do, though, right? But he's not up yet.'

Harry grinned. 'Yes, he is. I went in and woke him with a damp washcloth. He's already showered.'

'I'm impressed. Although I do prefer the way you wake *me* in the morning.'

'Yeah, that wouldn't impress my brother if I did that to him.'

'Did what to me?' Derek said as he came into the kitchen, a big smile on his face.

'Never you mind,' Harry said. 'Coffee, toast, then up the road.'

'Nae bother. I had a great sleep last night.'

'Don't you have a great sleep every night? You don't work, you go to bed late and sleep in every morning.'

'I plan on being a busy man from now on.'

'Do tell.' Harry buttered his own toast and took a mug of coffee after the kettle switched off.

'Briony and I are going into business together.'

'Doing what?' Alex asked.

'Yeah, doing *what*?' Harry said, and Alex threw him a warning look. 'I'm just asking.'

'We have to fine tune things, but Bobby was a businessman and he had a few irons in the fire. Briony has a head for those things.'

'Just be careful what you get into. Remember, she wants to kick our mother out into the street.'

'Everybody was emotional. Briony will be on speaking terms with her in no time.' Derek took a mug of coffee.

'Even after Ma's living in a cardboard box.'

'That's not going to happen. Ma will just have to move back into her own place. It just needs a little bit of TLC. She'll be fine.'

Harry looked at his watch. Just after eight thirty. 'We better get a move on. And you, dear brother, better call an Uber or plan on getting a bus.'

Sylvester the cat came through and meowed at

them. 'Oh crap, I nearly forgot to feed the cat,' Harry said.

'Don't worry, he's already been fed,' Alex said, picking him up. 'Auntie Alex has to go to work, but we'll be back later.'

Downstairs, Derek said he would get a bus up to Waverley station where he would catch a train to Dalmeny. 'I tried calling Ma but there's no answer. She's maybe still asleep. I need her to pick me up at the station. Those cabbies get their vest in a ruffle when the fare is two minutes and only costs a few quid.'

'At least it's something for them,' Alex said.

'They worry that they'll get a fare that takes two minutes and the next person to come along wants to go to Inverness or something and they'd miss out on a big earner.'

'I'll call her from the car and let her know you're coming.'

'If she answers.'

'I'll keep trying. You keep trying too.'

'I will. Thanks for letting me stay. You too, Alex.' He gave her a hug and shook Harry's hand. He started walking along the pavement then stopped just as Harry got the car door open.

'Do this again?'

Harry nodded. 'We'll do it again.'

He got into the car and drove it away.

'Something died in here,' Alex said. 'I wish we hadn't agreed on alternate days for using our cars.'

'Will wee Rory be greetin' today because we didn't take him out?' He looked across at her bright red Audi A3 sitting opposite outside the bowling club.

'*She*. Rosie hates you. She hates when you get in her seat and start fiddling with the radio and the seat position.'

'Rosie the Red Audi. Please don't say that out loud to anybody.'

'I tell people you named her. They think you're daft anyway so they just smile and nod in a *poor Harry* way.'

'You're going to marry me, and I'm the daft one? What will they think of you after that?'

'That never occurred to me. They'll think I'm as daft as you.'

Harry took his phone out and dialled his mother's number. 'No answer,' he said, disconnecting.

'Your mother's retired. She doesn't have to get up early like we do.'

'Are you kidding? Old people don't sleep in. They get up at the crack of dawn. They seize the day, not languish around in bed like us lazy young people.'

'She probably went out shopping or something.'

Harry carried on up towards Queensferry Road and Blackhall, only five minutes from where they were.

'I'm worried about her,' he said, cutting along the side street that would lead down to Michelle Naismith's street.

'Because Derek thinks your mother is a mass

murderer? Does he think that she's away out to the local Tesco with an axe? I like Derek a lot, but I think his imagination got away with him.'

'Me too.' His voice didn't sound too confident when he spoke.

They parked opposite Michelle Naismith's house and Harry knocked on the door. They could see a figure rising up from the floor through the opaque glass panels in the door.

When Michelle opened the door, she looked flustered.

'I hope we didn't catch you at a bad time?' Harry said.

'Just cleaning up my dead husband's blood from the floor,' she said. They could see the bucket on the hall floor. 'I'd shake your hand but as you can see...' She waved a yellow Marigold glove in their faces.

'We need to talk to you, Mrs Naismith,' Alex said, feeling sorry for the woman. She knew she would be grief-stricken if she lost Harry.

'Oh well, such is life. I suppose you better come in. I can get the kettle on and get some fairy cakes out if you give me time to get the remainder of my husband's guts off the floor.' She closed the door behind them.

Harry could see most of the crime scene detritus had already been cleaned but knew there was always little bits left behind. It hardly looked like a murder scene now, but he could see little specks of blood still.

'Where's the family liaison officer?' Harry asked.

'Her? Useless. I told her not to come back. Please go through to the living room.'

'After you,' Harry said.

She led them in and stood with her rubber gloves dripping onto the shag pile. 'Tea or coffee?'

'Sit down, Mrs Naismith,' Harry said, seeing the need to take control of the situation. Her son, Dennis, was sitting on the couch, staring into space.

She sat down like a scolded schoolgirl, looking at them with a mixture of impatience and shock.

'You okay, son?' he said, but the boy just stared ahead.

'It's hit him really hard, losing his stepdad.'

'I know this is hard for you, but you have all the help you need,' Alex said.

'Really? Help with taking Rachel to school, or helping Dennis with his football practice, driving him to the games? Help with the shopping? Or doing odd jobs around the house? Stuff like that?'

'Somebody to talk to,' Harry said.

'Great. I can talk about how my husband was shagging around all the time. How he would go out on a Friday night and pull some slapper.'

'Did you know she was swapped at birth?' Harry said, wanting to get the question asked, having to get straight to the point.

Michelle looked at him like he had two heads. 'Of course she wasn't swapped at birth! Who told you such a thing?'

'Peter Michaels has taken the first step to getting his little girl exhumed. She died when she was a month old. She had a heart defect. Just like your first child.'

'What the hell are you talking about?'

'We know that your little boy died,' Alex said.

'What has that got to do with things?' Michelle's face creased with anger.

'Peter Michaels was the man who's been watching your house. You reported seeing a man standing in the park, watching the house. Dennis managed to get a photo of him, and we traced him. His daughter died, and we believe that she was actually your daughter, swapped at birth.'

'Why would he swap the babies?'

'We don't think he did. But he found out.'

Michelle was silent for a moment. 'Do you think he was the one who killed Clark? I saw somebody running down the road.'

'No, we don't think he killed your husband. I just wanted to reassure you that the man who was watching your house isn't a psychopathic killer.'

'For God's sake, how do you know?'

'Because after he left the scene here, he and his wife drove to a petrol station and the internal security cameras captured his image, and he didn't have a speck of blood on him. We had his car impounded and forensics are going over it, and their initial findings are, no blood. Anywhere in the car. And trust me, the way your husband was brutally stabbed, there would have been transference. There's not one bit of evidence to show that it's even been cleaned.'

'Do you have any leads at all?' Michelle looked between them, waiting for the answer.

'Do you know anybody called Bobby Dixon?' Harry asked.

'I know *of* him.'

'Can you tell me how?'

Michelle took a deep breath before carrying on. 'He was a client of Clark's. Clark did some work for him when Dixon wanted a business loan. Sometimes a loan officer has to go and look at plans, or where something is being built, that sort of thing. Clark went to meet Dixon, and for some reason, they hit it off. They became friends.'

'How long ago was this?' Alex asked.

'About six years ago.'

Harry looked surprised. 'All that time?'

'Yes. Dixon used the Scottish National bank for all his banking and he took out a lot of business loans. Clark didn't go into a lot of details of course, but they became friends and socialised.'

'Was Clark friends with Dixon's daughter, Briony?' Alex asked.

'Yes, he was. I didn't have much time for her and I never socialised with Dixon. Frankly, I don't know what Clark saw in him. Or her. She was a nurse, I remember that. She worked in the maternity ward when I was there giving birth to... Rachel.' She seemed to think about it. 'I don't believe she's not mine. A mother knows.'

'What about your other job?' Harry asked. 'That's something you didn't tell us about.'

'What about it? I'm not a prostitute. I know there are escort agencies that provide that sort of service, but that's not what Arthur Daniels supplies. We really do just go out to social occasions and the like. And we don't go home with them. Why is that important?'

'Somebody might have taken a shine to you and decided to kill your husband to get him out of the way before making his move on you. It's happened before; get rid of the rival, paving the way.'

'Oh my God. You don't think that's what happened to Clark, do you?' She put her yellow-gloved hand on her chest for a moment.

'That's what we want to ask you; did any of the men pester you? Or contact you after your date with them?'

'They don't get my contact details. And we use an alias, so they don't know our real names.'

'You've never had any problems?'

'None at all.'

Harry looked at the boy sitting on the settee. 'Are you sure your son is okay?'

'He's had a sedative. Just to calm him down a bit.'

'Did the doctor come and give it to him?' Alex asked.

'No. They were mine. I took them after my parents

died. I know how much to give him though. My sister's a nurse so she kept me right.'

'She's a nursing assistant in a nursing home though, isn't she?'

'She used to be a nurse in the Royal. The stress got to her so she switched careers.'

'We talked to Linda about your parents,' Harry said. 'That was an unfortunate situation. It's never easy when a loved one decides...'

'Spare me the lecture, Inspector. They were a pair of selfish bastards.'

Harry knew people worked through their grief in stages, anger being one of them.

'Anyway, we just wanted to come and tell you that the man you saw standing in the park isn't the man who killed your husband. However, the killer is still on the loose so please still use caution. I can have the FLO come back any time. She can stay with you.'

'I'm more than capable of looking after myself.'

There was silence for a moment before Harry and Alex stood.

'You can call me any time, night or day, if you want to talk. If you remember anything else.'

'You'll be the first one I call.' She stood up beside them. 'Dennis, say goodbye.'

The boy moved his eyes and blinked a couple of times before looking away again.

'He'll be fine. This has hit him pretty hard.'

'How's your daughter?' Harry asked.

'She's in school. She's upset too, of course, but I think the younger ones adapt more easily, don't they?'

'Sometimes they do. What school does she go to?'

'The primary across the road, just past the park.'

'Keep your eye on her. Sometimes it takes longer for the shock to hit the younger ones,' Harry said.

'I will.'

They walked out to the front door, skirting the area where technicians had crawled round, taking swabs of everything. Harry could see some spots of blood but didn't want to point it out.

'Talk to you soon,' he said.

'Hopefully with news of Clark's killer,' she said and gently closed the door behind them.

'She's a real charmer,' Harry said as he got back behind the wheel of the Mondeo.

'She's been through a lot. First her folks kill themselves, then her husband gets murdered on her doorstep. Only months apart. It would break me.' Alex belted herself in.

'I know, but you saw the state of that laddie; he looks like he's been hit with an elephant tranquiliser.'

'Poor kid,' Alex said.

'I want to go to the mortuary to have a look at the parents' death reports.'

'Why?'

Harry looked at her. 'What if somebody is out to get Michelle Naismith and they started out by killing her parents?'

'Christ, that's a scary thought, Harry.'

'There is one thing that's niggling me though.'

'What's that?'

'Michelle said she saw a man running down the road after Clark was stabbed.'

'Right.'

'We've identified him as Peter Michaels. So if that was him, where did the killer go?'

'Good point.'

Before Harry started driving, his phone rang. He looked at the screen. It was his brother.

'Derek. What's up?'

'Harry! Christ almighty. Oh my God.'

'Calm down, Derek. What's going on?' A sudden feeling of dread hit him then, along with a shot of adrenaline.

'It's Mum. She's not here, Harry.'

'She knew you were staying overnight though, didn't she?'

'Yes. But that's not my point. There's blood on the kitchen floor and her car's still in the garage. I checked the house and she's not here. I asked our next-door neighbour and they saw nothing.'

'How much blood?'

'More than just a couple of drips from a bleeding nose. But get this; there's a bloody handprint on the doorframe leading to the garage.'

'Where's Briony?'

'At work.'

'Where's work?'

'The Royal in Edinburgh. She was working late last night. She often doesn't get finished on time.'

'I'm on my way over. Text her number to Alex.'

'Okay. Hurry, for God's sake.'

Harry switched the blues on behind the front grill and hit the siren after doing a three-point turn. He roared away towards Queensferry Road. Then he hit the button on the steering wheel to make a call.

'DI Keen? It's DCI Harry McNeil. I need you to go to this address. I'll meet you there. I'm coming over right now.' He told Keen his mother's address.

'Okay, sir, I'll make my way over there now.'

'My brother's already there. I think my mother might have been attacked in her home and taken.'

'I'll make it a priority, sir.'

Harry hung up and called another number. 'Ronnie? It's McNeil. I need you to go to the mortuary for me. Check up on something.' He told DI Vallance what he wanted.

'I'll get right onto it, sir.'

Harry disconnected the call and put his foot down when he reached the main road. He was glad he'd kept the lights and sirens on the car as he hit the outside lane.

Now he believed his brother's story about Bobby Dixon being murdered.

TWENTY-FOUR

'How you liking being in MIT?' Ronnie Vallance said as the car's engine was switched off.

'I like it, sir. There's more of a challenge,' Eve Bell said. Wind was blowing down through the Cowgate on its way to Holyrood Palace, making the city mortuary seem even more bleak.

'Stick with it. It's the younger generation like you who'll be running Police Scotland one day. Me? I love my job but there's not so much opportunity for me anymore. Harry McNeil is a rising star too. A DCI at forty. Good on him. He takes a lot of shite from people though because he was in Standards. Fuck 'em, that's what I say.'

'That's pretty much what I think. There are still a lot of dinosaurs in the force. Present company excepted.'

'What? I'll give you bloody dinosaur in a minute.'

She laughed as they went into the mortuary. Angie Patterson, one of the newer assistants, welcomed them in.

'Doctor Murphy is through in her office,' she said, leading them down a short corridor.

'Thanks, Angie,' Eve said.

'Knock, knock,' Vallance said, almost filling the doorway of the office.

Kate Murphy, one of the pathologists, looked up from her desk. 'Ronnie! I haven't seen you in a wee while. How have things been?'

'I've been keeping busy, Doctor Murphy. And now I'm part of Harry McNeil's team.'

'Excellent. I got the message that he wanted you to look at the records of two of my clients.' She made it sound like the dead people she cut up on a stainless-steel table were customers who were in to get fitted for an expensive watch.

'He wants you to look at the toxicology reports in particular.'

'Sit down, Ronnie. You too, Eve. I have them right here.'

The two detectives sat down on the opposite side. It wasn't a big office and there was hardly any room for two more chairs, but Vallance did his best to squeeze in without looking like he was sucking his gut in.

There were no papers on the desk. Kate saw him looking. 'The twenty-first century, Sherlock,' she said, smiling. She swung the flat screen monitor around for them to see.

'I knew that.'

'This is the post-mortem report. As you can see, there were some scrapes on the mother's leg. Nothing to write home about. She could have scraped herself anywhere, even against the side of a cabinet door that had been left open. There were no signs of violence. Nothing on the father. The police investigation showed they had both taken sedatives before climbing into their car and connecting a hosepipe to the exhaust and putting it through the rear passenger window in their garage.'

'Wait,' Vallance said. 'Sedatives? I thought it was sleeping tablets.'

Kate turned the screen round and brought up another page. 'I was looking at it before you came in. Let me double-check.' She looked at him. 'Making me doubt myself. Don't you dare ask me if I switched my gas oven off this morning.'

'Wouldn't dare. You did lock your front door though, didn't you?'

'Shut up, Vallance. I swear to God, if I have to leave here and go home at lunchtime...' She smiled as she found what she was looking for. 'There you go; they both had Valium in their system. Three times the amount that would normally be prescribed for a daily dose. But they obviously wanted to make sure they were asleep when the fumes started coming into the car.'

'In other words, they had the means to kill themselves without using the car,' Eve said.

'Yes. I have a list of medications removed from the house for comparison at the lab. There was only one medication bottle without a label and that had the Valium in it.'

'They could have taken the whole lot. I'm assuming there was quite a bit more in the bottle if it was taken away for comparison?' Vallance said.

'Yes. There were another twenty tablets in there. They could have split the whole lot between them and laid down on the bed and the outcome would have been the same.'

'Thanks, Kate,' Vallance said, standing up before the cheap office chair gave him cramps.

'No problem.'

They left the mortuary and got back in the car. 'Why would they take so much Valium only to kill themselves in the car?' Vallance said as Eve started the car.

'Only one reason I can think of; it was to incapacitate them before putting them in the car to make it look like suicide. I think somebody murdered Michelle Naismith's parents. And now they've murdered her husband.'

TWENTY-FIVE

DI Matt Keen walked down the front steps of Margaret O'Neil's house in Dalgety Bay. He wore a wax jacket over his suit, protection against the wind that was howling in off the Forth.

There were several patrol cars parked and a crime scene van.

'You brother's inside with my sergeant, sir,' Keen said as Harry and Alex got out of the car and walked towards him. Harry didn't feel the cold because his body felt like it was going to explode like a dying star.

'Take me to him.' It sounded more like *Take me to your leader* he thought but the words had already escaped his lips.

Inside, the central heating was battling with the cold that was coming through the open front door.

'Jesus, Harry,' Derek said, rushing over to him. 'This guy thinks I killed Ma.'

Keen shook his head. 'It's standard procedure, sir.' He then looked at Harry. 'There's blood in the dining room. Round a chair that was pulled away from the dining table. There's rope on it, like somebody was tied up and beaten. The rope was then cut, it looks like, and the person taken away.

They heard a commotion from the downstairs entrance.

'It's my fucking hoose, ya arsehole,' Briony Dixon said, making an entrance. She came up the stairs and into the large living room.

'Derek! Thank God you're alright. What's going on?'

'I would have called, but you had sent a text saying you were on your way home and I didn't want you to drive like a maniac. Any more than usual.'

Briony was about to protest but let it slide, no doubt keeping it in the bank for a future date. 'Tell me what's happened.'

'We think my mother was tied up and beaten in the dining room. Then somebody took her.'

'What? Who would do that?'

'We were hoping you could tell us,' Alex said.

'You don't think it was me?'

'We have two suspects,' Keen said. 'Those closest to the lady in question. And since you both live here, well, that puts you at the top of the suspect list until we can rule you out.'

'I can vouch for my brother,' Harry said. 'He spent the night with us at our flat.'

Briony shook her head. 'I was at work all night. In the Royal. I work in the maternity unit. I never left all night. I was too damn busy. I even finished work late and I just drove over here. It took me about half an hour.'

'We'll have to check that out, of course,' Keen said.

'Please do.'

'Get one of your people on it right away, Keen. I want Briony's alibi checked out right now,' Harry said. He turned to Derek. 'Did you look through the whole house when you came in?'

'Yes. Everywhere. Every room, even the garage. Her car is still there, Bobby's Jag too.' Derek looked down at the carpet for a moment before looking back at Harry. 'Because they weren't married, Briony is Bobby's next of kin. She already owned the house, but she got Bobby's money and belongings, which included his car. I'm sorry.'

'There's nothing to be sorry about. It is what it is. For whatever reason they didn't get married, Briony is entitled to get what's rightly hers. I can't fault her for that.'

Briony turned to him. 'I wasn't going to kick your mother out into the street. What I didn't tell you was, I had paid a decorator to go in to your mum's house and get it looking new. A contractor's been in and fixed a few little jobs that needed doing. Your mum was going to be comfortable and we would still be here, five minutes away from her. You can check if you like.'

'That's very kind of you,' Harry said.

She stepped closer to him. 'I was a bitch, Harry, but emotions were running high. Derek told me he thought my dad was murdered.'

'Did he tell you who he thought it was?' He looked at his brother who very slightly shook his head.

'No, he didn't say why he thought this.' Briony turned to Derek. 'Do you have any ideas?'

'No, none at all. I think I'm just naturally suspicious, since my dad was a copper, and my brother.' He looked away. Harry didn't mention Derek's thoughts about their mother being a potential murderer, and he dismissed all thoughts of that. He did now think that maybe Bobby Dixon had been murdered, but not at the hands of Harry's mother.

His phone rang in his pocket. He took it out and answered it, walking away to the window.

'Ronnie, what you got?'

'Harry, you're not going to believe this, but Eve and I think Michelle Naismith's parents were murdered. They had enough Valium in their blood to kill them, but then they decided to go into a car and gas themselves? Now, I obviously don't know how long it took them before they got to the car of course, but the longer time passes, the more likely it was they would start to feel drowsy.'

'Somebody could have forced the pills down their

throat to make it easier to manipulate them. That way, the toxicology report shows the sedatives but nobody puts two and two together. Very clever. Make it look like suicide.'

'That's exactly what we were thinking.'

'Ronnie, get onto DI Shiels. Get her and Simon Gregg to go and check up on the sister. I believe she was doing nights, so she should be in. Get them to try anyway. I'll have Alex text you the address. I want you and Eve to go and check on Michelle Naismith. If somebody has killed her parents and husband, then she might very well be a target herself. We were just with her, but I'm starting to think she could be a target. We'll take her into protective custody. Just in case.'

'I'll get right on it, boss.'

He hung up and didn't want to say anything in front of the others. Alex had her phone out and was sending a text.

He took her aside. 'The toxicology report on Michelle Naismith's parents showed a lethal amount of Valium in their system.'

'They would have died anyway?'

'Yes. But it seems like somebody wanted to make sure the job got done. When the Valium kicked in, they would be able to manipulate the couple.'

'Was there any sign of foul play at their house?' Alex asked.

'No. Nothing out of place. Maybe the killer tidied up, but there was not one thing out of place.'

'They were overpowered, maybe?'

'Could be. They were elderly, but not too old. But it's easy to overpower people with a weapon. But one thing niggles me; neither of them was prescribed Valium. Yet, there was one medication bottle without a label on it and that contained the Valium. No prints. Now, if it was theirs and they'd chosen to take the tablets, wouldn't you think their prints would have been on it?'

'Of course. So the killer brought a bottle of Valium with them? Christ, they were going to force the pills down them and get them into the car, and hope the post-mortem would show the sedatives but it wouldn't throw up a red flag. Very clever.'

'It was an attempt to fool the authorities – us – into thinking they were suicidal. And it worked, obviously. Whoever was called to the scene found them in the car and thought it was suicide. Why would the pathologist argue with that? It was in the toxicology report, but if they had other drugs in their system, why would it stick out? Especially if they had previously been to the doctors about anxiety. There was nothing jumping out to indicate this was anything other than suicide.'

'I wonder what the motive was then?'

'Somebody is out to take care of that family. It didn't start with Clark like we thought, but with Michelle's parents.'

'Sir?'

They all turned to look at a white-suited technician

standing at the door of the living room. He was holding up a little poly bag.

The detectives walked over.

'What is it?' Harry asked, but he knew what it was before the young woman spoke.

'It's a Valium pill. We found it in a corner of the dining room.'

TWENTY-SIX

Karen Shiels pulled the car into a parking spot in Oxgangs and Simon Gregg was out of it before the engine was off. Karen looked at her phone again, double-checking the address.

The two uniformed officers in the following patrol car got out and joined them.

'It's in here, Simon.' She pointed to the stair ahead of them.

Gregg nodded but didn't say anything. They strode into the stairway where it was dank. They heard raised voices, a TV playing loud and a dog barking. Maybe the dog didn't like daytime TV.

Gregg knocked on Linda Hogan's front door. 'I'm going to huff and puff and kick your door down,' he said after the third knock.

'Get it down,' Karen said to one of the uniforms.

The words were hardly out of her mouth before

the man's boot made contact with the door and it cracked back in against the wall.

Inside, the flat smelled of stale cooking and cigarette smoke. They checked the rooms but there was nobody home.

'It's empty,' one of them said.

'Get onto the emergency joiner and have the door secured.'

The man nodded and walked away, getting on his radio.

'What a hovel,' Gregg said. 'And this woman's a nurse?'

'Used to be. She works in a nursing home. Night shift. She was at work last night and should have been at home sleeping I would have thought. She got off at seven this morning.'

'Doesn't mean to say she didn't go somewhere for breakfast.'

Karen looked at her watch. 'How long does breakfast take? I mean, for somebody not as large as you.'

Gregg was six foot six and well-built but not overweight.

'I eat healthy. Just a bit of toast and a yoghurt.'

'Yeah, right. On top of the three bacon rolls.'

'I don't know what you've heard about me, but it's all gossip.' He had put his nitrile gloves on and moved some stuff around in the living room. He looked at a dining chair. There was a rope attached to it that had been cut. Now both ends hung limply round the legs from the chair back.

'Look at this,' he said, careful where he was putting his feet when he saw the blood.

Karen came over and looked at it. 'Jesus. I'll call DCI McNeil. Call this in, Simon. Get forensics out here.'

'Will do.' He walked away to make the call while Karen took out her own phone.

'DCI McNeil. We're at the sister's flat. We found rope on a chair that's been cut, like somebody had been tied to it before they were cut loose. There's also blood on the carpet round the chair.'

'Okay, get forensics in there. And start getting uniforms to go door-to-door to see if anybody's seen anything.'

'I'll get right onto it and I'll give you an update as soon as I know anything.'

She hung up. Then decided to call Ronnie Vallance to see how he was doing.

TWENTY-SEVEN

'You worked in Gayfield Square, didn't you?' Vallance said as Eve Bell expertly weaved through the heavy traffic in the city centre.

'I did, for a little while.'

'Did you work with Johnny Boy McGuire?'

She grinned. 'Oh yes. We had some good times, down at the police club.'

'Me too. I'm a big lad, mind...' he held up a finger and gave her a look, 'but Johnny Boy could put them away. And he was as thin as a bloody rake. Started to put a beer gut on though. Silly bastard left his wife for a barmaid recently.'

Eve took her eyes off the road for a moment. 'What? Away with yourself. Sir?'

'Bus.'

'What?'

'Mind that fucking bus.'

Eve navigated round it and Vallance thought he might have lost five pounds, he was sweating that much.

'Where did the barmaid work?'

Vallance was amazed at how cool she had stayed. She'd nearly had them under the wheels of a number 12 and hadn't missed a heartbeat. This detective was going far.

'The police club. She was one of the new ones. Christ knows why he decided to leave his wife for her. Johnny Boy's been married for over twenty years. Mid-life crisis, I think. His wife sometimes went away on business trips and Johnny said he got lonely. Most guys would call their mother to ask how to microwave a dinner in a box, but oh no, Johnny had to go the extra mile and spend more time in the club. Turns out, Nice but Dim Kim gave him more than a plate of chips. Now they're calling him Silly Boy McGuire. He doesn't care though; he thinks they're just jealous.'

'They probably are. And what a name to call her! Bunch of animals, calling a nice young woman that. Nice but Dim Kim, indeed.'

'Well, she's not the sharpest sausage in the butcher's window, that's for sure. Nice looking, but I prefer my woman to be smart first and foremost. Up here for thinking, down there for dancing, and don't get the two mixed up. I don't care how well coiffed Kim is, if she can't spell the name of an expensive lager, I would have given her a wider berth than the Queen Mary gives an iceberg.'

'She's good fun. We always have a laugh when we're in there and she's working.'

'She should have known better than to mess about with a married man, that's all I'm saying,' Vallance said, gripping the *Oh shit* handle a little tighter.

'I know what you're saying, but there had to have been a crack in his marriage to have let a young woman steal him away from his wife.' She sailed through a traffic light just as it had turned red.

'I think Johnny's always had a roving eye, but nobody's given him a second look until now. I mean, he's not a bad looking bloke, but a lot of women won't give a second look to a married man. Lucky I'm a big ugly bastard.'

'You're not bad looking, sir.'

'I'm not fishing for compliments, sergeant, just stating facts. I'm six three, weigh eighteen stone, need to go on a diet, have a big bush stuck to the front of my face and can lift two pint glasses from the top with one hand. I'm somebody only my wife could love and for that I'm thankful. I wouldn't throw all of it away just to end up in a scabby bedsit eating dog food on toast.'

'Has Johnny Boy messing around got to you?' Eve said as she went through another traffic light, green this time.

'This is not bloody Brands Hatch we're on, Eve. Cool your jets a bit there. Just because you're in pole position doesn't mean to say we want to test out the car's limits.' He looked out of the window as she shot down Morrison Street towards Haymarket station.

'Well, has it?' she asked again.

'I suppose it has. He and I would meet up there on a Tuesday night. That was our night for having a quiet couple of beers, you know? Catch up with things. And now that's all over.'

'I can understand that. It's almost like Kim has taken Johnny away from *you*, not just his wife.'

'Aye. That makes sense. I suppose she has in a way. Took my mate away from me.'

'I'm sure he'll still have a pint with you.'

'You would think, Eve, but that's not always the case. I call him up and sometimes she answers, and I can tell they've been drinking, and she'll talk some dirty stuff over the phone. To me! For fuck's sake. My missus would rip her into a thousand pieces if she heard Kim talking like that. God Almighty. I never thought a young lassie would have a mouth on her like that. But Johnny doesn't mind; he's forty-one and she's twenty-five.'

'Doesn't she have kids?'

'Aye, two ankle biters. Eight and five, he told me. I mean, Johnny's got two of his own kids. Twenty and seventeen. His son is the older one and he's been busting his dad's balls about Kim. The girl is more confused, asking how he could do this to them. What a right mess he's got himself into. You couldn't pay me enough to drop myself into the mire like that.'

Eve stopped the car opposite Michelle Naismith's house and they got out. The sky was the colour of slate and the temperature had dropped.

They were walking across the road when Vallance stopped on the pavement. 'Hold on. The door's open a crack.' They both instinctively took their extendable batons and walked up the path to the front door of the house. Vallance nudged it open with the boot and it swung in noiselessly.

'Mrs Naismith? It's the police! If you're here, make yourself known!'

They both extended their batons and moved in cautiously. The house was quiet, but they wouldn't expect an intruder to be running about, shouting.

'If he comes at us with a knife, let him have it. I'm not fucking about. He's already proved he's a killer.'

Vallance walked forward, Eve looking around them, her nerves like taut wire. They checked each of the rooms on the ground floor, then went up to the bedrooms. Rachel and Dennis were each lying in their own beds, unconscious.

'Call it in, Eve. I'll call Harry McNeil.'

She took her phone out and Vallance went into the living room to call Harry. Then he stopped dead. The dining table was at the back of the living room. Pieces of rope were hanging from the back of a chair. A washcloth lay on the table in front of the chair.

He stepped closer and looked at the pale blue washcloth. It had a dark stain on the front, which he was certain was blood.

He made the call. 'Harry? We've got a big problem.'

TWENTY-EIGHT

'What's wrong?' Derek said.

Harry put his phone away. They were still standing in the living room, more people bustling around them. Alex had left with a couple of uniforms a short time ago.

'Christ, Michelle Naismith and her sister are both gone.'

'Gone? Where?'

'There were ropes on chairs, at both of their places, like they'd been tied and beaten. Blood was at both locations.'

'Just like here. Good God.' Derek shook his head.

Briony was sitting down. 'Look, boys, I don't want to piss on anybody's parade, but why is your mother involved in this? Where does she fit in?'

Harry looked at her. He wouldn't be talking to her

if he thought she was involved, but a quick call to the Royal had confirmed her alibi.

'Derek here had heard Bobby arguing with Clark Naismith. He came here to the house and they had words.'

'He came here?'

'Yes. They were arguing downstairs and Bobby shut the door on him,' Derek said.

Briony looked at Harry. 'I know she's your mother, but do you think she could have been involved?'

It was like a punch to his guts. Harry felt strange inside. It wasn't until somebody had actually voiced it did he give consideration to the fact that his mother might be involved.

'I want to say no, but things are not looking so good.'

'Do you think she would have it in her to kill Clark Naismith?' Derek said.

'Maybe. If she thought he had killed Bobby. Some people are driven to it.'

Alex came back in and dashed up to Harry. 'I just looked at a neighbour's CCTV. I'm sorry to say, but your mother was caught on his camera reversing a car out of the driveway last night and driving away.'

Harry rubbed his face, trying to keep his thoughts straight and failing miserably. 'Number plate?'

Alex shook her head. 'We couldn't make it out. It was a Ford Focus, older model. That's all. It's a very grainy footage.'

'Why is there blood here? If my mother did this, who did she tie to a chair?'

Nobody had the answer, then another tech came into the room. 'There was a lock box in the wardrobe. It was unlocked and empty. Do you know if your mother had a passport?'

Harry nodded. 'Yes. She was in Tenerife over Christmas.'

The tech walked away.

'Get a trace on her bank card. She banked with the Royal,' Harry said to Matt Keen. Then a thought struck him.

'You said you were helping my mother get her place done up?' he said to Briony. 'When's the last time you were in there?'

'Ages. There's nobody living there just now. It was getting decorated.'

'Where are the keys?'

'In my chest of drawers,' she replied then turned and rushed out of the room. She returned two minutes later. 'They're gone.'

Harry turned to Keen. 'Get armed response. We're going to Rosyth.'

TWENTY-NINE

Harry led the convoy, knowing exactly where he was going. At high speed, it took less than ten minutes. Under the M90 motorway flyover, he drove straight on and floored it, towards the next roundabout where he turned right into Queensferry Road.

He'd driven here so many times in the past that he could do it blindfolded. He jumped on the brakes and hooked a right at Rosyth Methodist church and was in his mother's street.

Her house was on the left. A detached bungalow with a gravel driveway on the left, leading to a detached garage in the back. He pulled in, the armed response pulling in behind him. The armed officers jumped out as the other cars pulled in and DI Matt Keen jumped out of an unmarked car.

'I can't believe we're doing this,' Harry said to Alex.

'Me neither. But I'm right here beside you. Don't forget that.'

'I won't.'

'I love you, Harry McNeil.'

'Love you too.'

They stood back as uniforms ran up to the front door under the guidance of Matt Keen and one of them battered the door with the ram and then the armed officers were in. There were shouts as the house was cleared. Keen came back out a few minutes later.

'Nobody here, but you need to see this.' He motioned for Harry to enter the house after instructing the armed team to check the garage.

Inside the living room, there was no furniture, only the fixings of a painter and decorator. Keen led them through to the kitchen where he pointed to a notepad on the counter. Harry read it without touching it.

Dear Harry.

I knew you would search here so I wanted to leave you this note. I'm sorry, son, for not being brave enough to fight, but I'm too old. Michelle Naismith killed Bobby and she killed her husband. I have to go with her or she said she's going to kill you and Derek. I love you both.

Mum xxx

Harry read the note again and felt panic grip him. It was an alien feeling, something he managed to suppress normally, but seeing his mother's note made the room spin.

'I'm sorry, sir,' Keen said. 'Any idea where this Michelle Naismith could have taken your mother?'

Harry shook his head and moved aside to let Alex read the note.

'Oh, Harry, I'm so sorry. Oh my God. We need to try and find her.'

'I think Michelle killed her parents too. They were drugged with sedatives and put in their car and a hosepipe attached to the exhaust,' he explained to Keen. 'I don't know the motive.'

'We can ask her when we get her,' Keen said. 'Does she have any family we can ask where she might have taken your mum?'

'Her sister's been taken too, and my DI said there's nobody at the sister's house.'

'Michelle's parent's house,' Alex said, standing back from the mote.

'What?' Harry said.

'Derek said that Bobby tried to buy it but the parents died before he could sign the papers. What if she took your mum there? It's isolated, nobody would see them.'

'Let's check it out. Keen, stay here and supervise this scene. I'm going back over to Edinburgh.'

'Very good, sir.'

Harry and Alex went back to their car, after a uniform confirmed the garage was empty.

'You drive,' he said to her, throwing her the keys.

As she roared away, he got his phone out and called Ronnie Vallance.

'Ronnie? I think Michelle Naismith is behind this. It looks like she might have murdered her husband and she's taken her sister hostage. Along with my mother. I know her parents lived on the outskirts near Queensferry but I need you to get the address for me and make your way there. I don't want to send the cavalry in but I want them on stand-by.'

'I have the address here, Harry. I wanted to go and have a look at the house where the parents died so I copied it. I'll text it to you and I'll make my way there with the others.'

'Thanks. If you get there first, try and hold back. I don't want her spooked. But if you need to move in, do it.'

'We're still at the Naismiths' now. I'll get backup here.'

Harry sat back as Alex floored the Mondeo, the lights and siren cutting through the traffic as she headed south on the M90, flying over the Queensferry Crossing, the new bridge spanning the Forth.

A few seconds later, his phone dinged and he opened it. The address from Ronnie. He called him and kept in contact. The house was a little place in the middle of the countryside, up from Kirkliston.

Vallance was giving Harry updates every thirty seconds or so: driving past the former army base at Craigiehall; middle of nowhere; turning right into another country lane; Christ, we're lost; no, we're not; turn left here, Eve! Mind that bloody Discovery! The bastard's driving like a maniac!

Harry told Alex to hold back. She had already cut the siren and Eve slowed their car down as she came up on them.

'It's down this single road, only about a couple of hundred yards away,' Harry said, as Alex slowly drove down.

They stopped before the entrance to the detached house. It wasn't particularly large, but there were several long buildings on the property, seemingly rundown. Harry told Vallance to get Eve to park up. This was as far as they went in the cars.

They got out, nobody slamming the doors shut.

'Ronnie,' Harry said. 'Michelle's got my mother. We need to get to her.'

'I've got backup right behind me. They're holding back but they're just outside, waiting to move in.'

'We have to do this quickly but I don't want to spook her.'

'Lead the way, boss.'

The sky was full of rain but was keeping it back while it blew some wind into them first, buffeting the trees on the property. There were two old, long buildings with open barn doors. Nothing in them. The house came into sight.

There was a double garage next to it, and Harry presumed this was where the parents had died.

'I can check out the garage,' Eve said. Harry nodded.

The front door of the house was open. Harry, Alex and Vallance walked forward. Harry entered first, preparing for a fight with Michelle Naismith.

'Her sister's missing, too,' Eve said. 'Maybe she brought Linda here first before bringing your mum.'

'Maybe. For God's sake, be alert.'

There wasn't a sound except birds from outside. Traffic in the distance. Nothing from the house.

The ground floor was empty so Harry started up the stairs, and that's when he smelled it.

Petrol.

He walked along the landing and was about to look into a room when he felt something brush his leg, and too late, he knew in an instant what was happening.

'Get out!' he ordered.

The other two detectives turned and ran. They hadn't seen what Harry had seen; Michelle Naismith hanging by a rope that was tied somewhere unseen in the attic. In the room beyond her, a figure with a what appeared to be a nursing uniform on, lay on a bed, a knife sticking out of her chest, a pillow over her face. Linda Hogan, Michelle's sister. Harry assumed.

But Harry knew what had touched his leg through his trousers, causing him to shout a warning to the others.

Fishing line.

He knew something was tied to one end of the line,

something that was going to set fire to the petrol-soaked carpet. A candle most likely. As he turned, he heard the whoosh and the flames licked out of the room on his right, the blue flame running across the carpet to the room where Linda lay dead.

The flames caught hold of Michelle's clothing and went up in an instant.

Ronnie Vallance made sure Eve was in front of him as they ran down the stairs, trying to protect her. Harry was right behind them and they reached the bottom just as flames exploded upstairs and began to make their way down the stairway.

When they got outside, windows started exploding. They kept moving away from the house.

Alex came running over from the direction of the garage.

Harry! What's going on?'

He grabbed hold of her. 'The place was rigged to go up. Everywhere was soaked with petrol.'

'Jesus, you could have died. Was Michelle in there?'

'She looked dead or not far off it. She was hanging out of the attic. Her sister was lying on a bed with a knife sticking out of her.' He looked at her. 'What about the garage? Is my mum there?'

Alex's lips started trembling and tears started running down her face. 'I'm so sorry, Harry.'

He felt himself go rigid as a wave of disbelief hit him. 'God, no, please.'

Alex grabbed him and pulled him close, holding on tight. Then he cried, hard, burying his face in her shoulder.

Sirens cut through the air, heading towards them.

And the house kept on burning, taking his mother's killer with it.

THIRTY

Alex knocked on Harry's office door and walked in. 'I've just been on the phone with the undertaker and they want you and Derek to go in and get an obituary made up for your mum.'

He nodded. 'Thanks, love. I don't know what I'd do without you.'

'Just promise me you'll be there for me one day, Harry. In *my* hour of need.'

'I'll be there, right by your side.'

It had been two days since the fire and discovering Margaret's corpse in the car in the garage and Harry still felt the weight of the world on his shoulders. Derek was a wreck but Briony was looking after him. His head had been spinning; first they'd thought his mother was a killer, then the note at her house said Michelle Naismith was the killer.

Things weren't adding up but he and the team had

debriefed and Vallance said that he thought Michelle had made Margaret write the note so they would figure out where she had taken them, so they would be found. In one way, it was a relief to think his mother wasn't a killer after all.

'I need to talk to you about something,' Alex said.

'What's that?'

'The forensics report. It's a preliminary just now, but they started with the garage as that's where the fire hadn't reached. I don't know if she had intended that part to go up, but there was no petrol in there. However, there *was* petrol on the wellington boots found in there, in front of the car your mum was found in.'

Harry looked blank for a moment, as if he had been miles away. 'Meaning?'

'Meaning they were wet, Harry. They had petrol on them. How would they be wet with petrol if Michelle was hanging in the house? I mean, why would she even bother to put wellies on if she was going to kill herself? Did she put them on, take them off in the garage and then go back inside in bare feet?'

Harry didn't say anything for a moment then shot forward in his chair. 'She was wearing shoes. Trainers. She had white trainers on with that Nike logo. I remember looking at them as I was going to try and lift her up to take the pressure off her neck. But then I hit the fishing line. But I remember the shoes.'

'She either went down to the garage after pouring

the petrol about and put shoes on so she could hang herself, or...'

'Or somebody else was there. Making it look like Michelle was a murderer.'

'I'm not saying that is the case, but if it is, we need to find out who.'

He sat back in his chair. 'Might as well toss a coin.'

'Maybe not,' Eve Bell said, coming over. 'Sorry, I couldn't help but overhear. I did a little digging, because I was curious, and Clark Naismith had a life insurance policy out on him. And the beneficiary wasn't his wife.'

'Who was it?'

She put the sheet of paper down on his desk. Harry looked at it then stood up, grabbing his jacket off the back of his chair.

THIRTY-ONE

Alex drove her Audi to the Royal Infirmary. Harry said he still felt numb and his mind kept going back and forth between thoughts of his mother and trying to focus on work. It had been made difficult with Commander Jeni Bridge wanting no stone left unturned, and even going as far as to run a scenario where Harry's mother was the killer and had placed the petrol-splashed boots in the garage before taking her own life, but after detailed forensic analysis, there wasn't the slightest trace of petrol on Margaret or inside the car. Plus, she was hardly likely to stab herself in the back, leave the knife there and put herself in the boot. Besides, where the knife was located meant it was impossible for Margaret to stab herself. She was murdered, pure and simple.

Harry was aghast, but his professionalism kicked in and he knew his colleagues had a job to do while he had to take a step back. Today though, he was front and centre.

Alex parked up and they went into the hospital, which was warm and a welcome relief from the cold outside. Spring was mocking them now, teasing them with decent temperatures one day before blasting them with a chill the next.

They made their way to the maternity wing. Harry had called Derek before coming here, just to make sure.

Briony Dixon came out to meet them. 'Hello, Harry. Alex. Is this about your mum's funeral?'

Harry shook his head. 'No, it's about something else entirely. Is there somewhere private we can talk?'

'Sure. There's a little break room we can use if there's nobody in it.' She led them down a corridor and stopped at a door, looking through the glass panel. 'It's empty.'

Inside, they sat down away from the vending machines.

'Would you like a coffee?' Briony asked.

'No,' Harry replied. He locked eyes with her for a moment. 'We don't know how you were involved in my mother's death, but I'm going to find out. I wanted you to know that.'

Briony sat back in the big vinyl chair as if she'd been slapped. 'What? What do you mean? I wasn't involved!'

'We have a copy of Clark Naismith's insurance

policy,' Alex said, taking it out of her pocket and unfolding it before handing it over. 'You're the sole beneficiary. Not his wife, not his kids, you.'

'Me? Why would I be the beneficiary of Clark's insurance payout? Surely his wife would have been the beneficiary?'

'Nope. As you can see for yourself, it's you. And it's already been paid out. They asked for a report and somebody sent them one saying you weren't a suspect in the case because you had an iron-clad alibi.'

Briony shook her head as she looked at the piece of paper in her hand. 'I know nothing about this. Why would Clark leave me the money? I hardly knew him.'

'I don't think that's quite true, do you?'

'I don't have half a million in my account.' She took her phone out and opened her banking app. A couple of minutes later, she sat stony-faced and held out the phone for Harry to see. 'Oh my God. What's going on here, Harry?'

'Is your name the only one on that account?' he asked, thinking he already knew the answer.

'No.'

Harry looked at Alex then back at Briony. 'This is what we're going to do.'

THIRTY-TWO

Briony sat in the darkened living room, sipping at her second glass of wine, her nerves getting steadier. She would never tire of looking at this view, at the twinkling lights of Edinburgh across the water, at the rail bridge in all her glory.

She was looking at the road that was the only way in and the only way out by car. On her left was a pathway that connected two streets. She didn't look that way, despite how tempting it might be. She started shaking again but managed to get the glass to her mouth without spilling a drop.

Then she held it there, listening hard. She thought she heard a sound, coming from downstairs. *Had the front door just opened?* She couldn't be sure though, like when people hear a noise through the night.

Then she heard it again, like the door had just been closed very quietly. She swallowed hard, putting the glass down on the little table. She had liked this house at first, with the front door being on the ground floor and having to come upstairs to the big living room, but now it felt as though she was trapped.

There was the faintest creak on the stairs, like somebody knew where most of the creaky steps were and was trying to avoid them.

Then the black-clad figure stepped into the room and stood looking across at her. He wore a ski mask

Briony looked at him. 'Hello, Dad.'

The figure took the ski mask off and grinned. 'Hello, darlin',' Bobby Dixon said. 'You don't look surprised to see me.' He stepped forward, getting closer.

'I figured I would see you after I transferred the half million out of our joint account into my own.'

'How did you know I was still alive?' The smile was still in place.

'It doesn't take a rocket scientist to figure it out when you left all the puzzle pieces behind.'

'I always said you were the brains in the family.'

'Not Clark?'

Dixon smiled. 'You found out? Obviously.'

'About him being my brother? Yes.'

'Half-brother, Briony.'

'Why didn't you ever tell me about him?'

'And ruin the little illusion you had about me? I

don't think so. You always had me on a pedestal when you were a wee girl.'

She looked at him with contempt. 'Until I met and married Ray.'

The smile fell from Dixon's face. 'I told you he was no good for you. I mean, he tried to be a replacement for me!' He tapped himself in the chest.

'He was a hard worker. That's how we got this place.'

'It was paid off when he died. He hardly worked for it.'

'He was more of a man than you.'

Dixon laughed. 'Please. He couldn't take my place.'

'What about Clark? He was your child too. Did you murder your own child?'

Dixon laughed. 'No, I didn't kill him. I had help with that.'

Briony wasn't sure she was seeing things correctly when the black shadow moved in the hallway just outside the living room, then the person walked in, dressed in black, just like Dixon.

'You two don't need any introductions,' Dixon said, turning to the figure.

'It was me who killed Clark,' Linda Hogan said, grinning.

'I helped too, of course,' Dixon said. 'I ran off down the road, taking the murder weapon with me. In the opposite direction to that idiot who had been watching the house.'

'The one who you stole a baby from? That was you, wasn't it, Linda? You and I both worked there at the time. Yet, you were the one who helped Clark swap babies.'

'Clark introduced me to Bobby as his real father and we hit it off. Clark had been drinking one night and told Bobby all about Michelle's first baby, who died. He was convinced this one would be the same. Turns out, he was right.'

'Then I had the idea of swapping the babies,' Dixon said. 'If they both survived, then both would have parents. Unfortunately, Linda found out that the other parents who now had Michelle's baby, lost her. She lived for one month and one day. Clark was devastated, but he had the other baby now, and they brought her up as their own, and nobody knew the difference. Only me, Linda and Clark knew.'

'Until the fight,' Linda said.

'What fight?' Briony asked.

'Between me and my parents. They always looked down on me. I lived in a crap hole because I drank my money away. Unlike Michelle, who had the perfect life. I told them about their granddaughter, who wasn't really their granddaughter. They were furious and were going to have it out with Clark.'

'But I couldn't have that. I was using Clark's position in the bank to get details of tenders of construction jobs. Those businesses who bank there of course. And Clark was quite happy to help me. I'd helped him with the baby after all. But with his snotty-nosed parents-in-law digging up the dirt, I wanted rid of them. And with the help of my new girlfriend, I did just that,' Dixon said.

Briony looked disgusted. 'You killed your own parents? How could you?'

Linda shrugged. 'It was easy. I'll do anything for Bobby. You know what a crap hole I live in. Bobby and I are going to live the high life now. They think I died in the fire with my sister, but by the time they find out, we'll be long gone.'

'Who was it?'

'Just some woman I befriended at the nursing home. Her mother's there. We became friends, so I could use her in our plan.'

Bobby smiled and stepped closer. 'And, daughter dear, you would have been fine if you hadn't transferred that money.'

'Don't you think I would have noticed you taking it out?'

He laughed. 'By that time, we'd be well away. However, we can all walk away from this if you just transfer it back.'

'I'm not doing that. Good God, helping a pair of killers? Did you have to kill Harry McNeil's mother?'

'She was just a pastime anyway. My real girlfriend is here. Margaret was fun for a while, but she was just in the way. Never leave witnesses. Clark was going to stop helping me and tell people what had been going on. He was stupid. I would have been ruined and I would have gone to prison.'

'You still are,' a voice said from behind him. Bobby and Linda spun round. Then Bobby smiled before addressing Briony.

'Very well played. Have Harry here hide in the house and get me to tell you what happened. Well, that's going to be another corpse they'll find. Might as well get hung for a sheep as a lamb, as the saying goes.'

'How did you fake your own death?' Harry asked.

Bobby shrugged. 'He was a friend of mine. I got somebody to get me into the dentist's office and I swapped dental records. You wouldn't even know I was there.'

He ran at Harry, who was only standing a few feet away now and they flew through the air as he crashed into him. For his age, or maybe it was desperation, Bobby could fight. But Harry was fuelled by hatred and pummelled his fists at Bobby's face.

Linda screamed and pulled out a knife and drew it back just as Alex ran at her, coming in from the hall. She had a baton in her hand and brought it down with such force, it broke Linda's arm and with another move, she had her in a headlock with it.

She looked sideways and saw Bobby was on top of Harry but then she heard what could only be described as a growl of pure and utter hatred.

Bobby rolled sideways and then the positions were reversed. Harry got on top of Bobby just as they heard sirens from outside. Harry pulled a knife out of his pocket and held it above his head.

'Sir!' DI Matt Keen shouted as he came into the room.

Harry brought the knife down hard.

THIRTY-THREE

Two weeks later

The wind blew in from the Moray Firth, making the sea a little bit choppy but Harry didn't feel it. He and Alex crossed the road from the little car park outside Fort George in Ardersier.

'My mother always said she wanted to spend her final days back where she was born, in Inverness,' he said, as he carried the stainless-steel urn in one hand.

'Last year, when we were travelling up north, I remember you telling me your granny was born here in Fort George and that you were born in Inverness,' Alex said, holding onto his free arm. 'I think your mum would be happy to know you were scattering her ashes here.'

'I think she would. I just wish Derek had wanted to come.'

'He's grieving in other ways, Harry. You can't blame him for not wanting to come here.'

'I don't. At least he wanted you to throw the wreath in.'

Alex was holding the circle of flowers that Derek had bought.

'I got a call from Jimmy Dunbar earlier. Dennis is back living with his father in Glasgow. And the latest I heard, social services are working to see if they can have young Rachel be placed into foster care with her biological parents. The Michaels are a decent couple. They would be delighted to get their daughter back, but it's going to be hard for the girl.'

'I hope it works out for them.'

They stood in silence for a moment, Harry looking at the hills in the distance across the body of water.

'You know, I think I might have rammed that knife into Bobby if Matt Keen hadn't shouted at me. I would have thrown my life away for Bobby Dixon and that would have been a waste.'

'I'm glad you stuck it into the floor. I would have missed the chance of being your wife if you'd killed him.'

'He wasn't worth it. He'll rot in prison, like Linda Hogan.'

They made their way down to the water and the

sun came out from behind some clouds, shining down on the sea.

'See? She's looking down on us,' he said.

Alex couldn't hold back the tears and when Harry gave her the nod, she threw the wreath into the cold water.

Harry opened the urn and slowly poured his mother's remains into the sea.

'I love you, Mum. 'Til we meet again.'

Then he stood still with Alex putting an arm around his waist. They stood like that until another cloud came along and the sun went into hiding again.

AFTERWORD

As always, I don't do this journey alone and have a support team behind me, making my job a lot easier.

I would like to thank the undercover agents who double as my advance readers. I appreciate each and every one of you.

Thank you to my wife, Debbie, who entertains our dogs while I write. I have the easy job.

My website is getting there, honest! I know I still have to get the contact button sorted. I would love to hear from anybody who cares to write, I just have to get the technical side down pat. If you want to say Hi on Facebook, please feel free. That's where I lurk most. Oh, and I post photos of my dogs on Instagram. Sometimes the cats, too, but when I tell them I want a photo for social media, they're like, whatever.

Once again, a huge thank you to my editor, Melanie Underwood. She has tremendous patience!

If I could ask you to please leave a review that would be fantastic. As always, it helps out an author like me.

Harry will return in Blood and Tears.

All the best my friends.

John Carson
New York
February 2020

ABOUT THE AUTHOR

John Carson is originally from Edinburgh, Scotland, but now lives in New York State with his wife and family. And two dogs. And four cats.

website - johncarsonauthor.com
    Facebook - JohnCarsonAuthor
    Twitter - JohnCarsonBooks
    Instagram - JohnCarsonAuthor

Made in the USA
San Bernardino, CA
16 March 2020

65776694R00144